Books by Terry Pratchett

TRUCKERS*
DIGGERS*
WINGS*
THE CARPET PEOPLE*
ONLY YOU CAN SAVE MANKIND*
JOHNNY AND THE DEAD*
JOHNNY AND THE BOMB*
THE AMAZING MAURING AND HIS EDUCATED RODENTS*
GOOD OMENS (with Neil Gaiman)
STRATA
THE DARK SIDE OF THE SUN
THE UNADULTERATED CAT (with Gray Jolliffe)†
THE PRATCHETT PORTFOLIO (with Paul Kidby)†

The Discworld® Series
THE COLOUR OF MAGIC*
THE LIGHT FANTASTIC*
EQUAL RITES*
MORT*
SOURCERY*
WYRD SISTERS*
PYRAMIDS*
GUARDS! GUARDS!*
ERIC*†
MOVING PICTURES*
REAPER MAN*
WITCHES ABROAD*
SMALL GODS*
LORDS AND LADIES*
MEN AT ARMS*
SOUL MUSIC*
INTERESTING TIMES*
MASKERADE*
FEET OF CLAY*
HOGFATHER*

JINGO*
THE LAST CONTINENT*
CARPE JUGULUM*
THE FIFTH ELEPHANT*
THE TRUTH*
THIEF OF TIME*
NIGHT WATCH*

THE COLOUR OF MAGIC – GRAPHIC NOVEL
THE LIGHT FANTASTIC – GRAPHIC NOVEL
MORT: A DISCWORLD BIG COMIC
(with Graham Higgins)†
SOUL MUSIC: THE ILLUSTRATED SCREENPLAY
WYRD SISTERS: THE ILLUSTRATED SCREENPLAY
MORT – THE PLAY (adapted by Stephen Briggs)
WYRD SISTERS – THE PLAY
(adapted by Stephen Briggs)
GUARDS! GUARDS! – THE PLAY
(adapted by Stephen Briggs)
MEN AT ARMS – THE PLAY
(adapted by Stephen Briggs)
THE DISCWORLD COMPANION
(with Stephen Briggs)†
THE STREETS OF ANKH-MORPORK
(with Stephen Briggs)
THE DISCWORLD MAPP
(with Stephen Briggs)
A TOURIST GUIDE TO LANCRE
(with Stephen Briggs and Paul Kidby)
DEATH'S DOMAIN (with Paul Kidby)
NANNY OGG'S COOKBOOK
(with Stephen Briggs, Tina Hannan and Paul Kidby)
THE LAST HERO: A Discworld Fable
(illustrated by Paul Kidby)†

* also available in audio
† published by Victor Gollancz

THE DARK SIDE
OF THE SUN

Terry Pratchett

CORGI BOOKS

THE DARK SIDE OF THE SUN
A CORGI BOOK : 0552133264
9780552133265

Originally published in Great Britain by Colin Smythe Ltd

PRINTING HISTORY
Colin Smythe edition published 1976
NEL edition published 1978
Corgi edition published 1998

25 27 29 30 28 26 24

Set in 11/13pt Palatino by
Kestrel Data, Exeter, Devon.

Corgi Books are published by Transworld Publishers,
61–63 Uxbridge Road, London W5 5SA,
a division of The Random House Group Ltd,
in Australia by Random House Australia (Pty) Ltd,
20 Alfred Street, Milsons Point, Sydney, NSW 2061, Australia,
in New Zealand by Random House New Zealand Ltd,
18 Poland Road, Glenfield, Auckland 10, New Zealand,
in South Africa by Random House (Pty) Ltd,
Isle of Houghton, Corner of Boundary Road & Carse O'Gowrie,
Houghton 2198, South Africa,
and in India by Random House Publishers India Private Limited,
301 World Trade Tower, Hotel Intercontinental Grand Complex,
Barakhamba Lane, New Delhi 110 001, India.

Printed and bound in Great Britain by
Cox & Wyman Ltd, Reading, Berkshire.

Papers used by Transworld Publishers are natural, recyclable
products made from wood grown in sustainable forests.
The manufacturing processes conform to the environmental
regulations of the country of origin.

THE DARK SIDE
OF THE SUN

1

'Only predict.' Charles Sub-Lunar, from *The Lights In The Sky Are Photofloods*

In the false dawn a warm wind blew out of the east, shaking the dry reed cases.

The marsh mist broke into ribbons and curled away. Small night creatures burrowed hastily into the slime. In the distance, hidden by the baroque mist curls, a night bird screeched in the floating reed beds.

In one of the big lakes near the open sea three delicate white windshells hoisted their papery sails and tacked slowly towards the incoming surf.

Dom waited just beyond the breakers, two metres below the dancing surface, a thin stream of bubbles rising from his gill pack. He heard the shells long before he saw them. They sounded like skates on distant ice.

He grinned to himself. There would only be

one chance. Some of those pretty trailing tendrils were lethal. There might never be another chance, ever. He tensed.

And knifed upwards.

The shell bucked violently as he grabbed the blunt prow, and he swung his legs hard over to avoid hitting the dangling green fronds. The world dissolved into a salt-tasting, cold white bubble of foam. Small silver fish slipped desperately past him, and then he was lying across the upper hull.

The shell had gone berserk, flailing with the bony mast in great slow sweeps. Dom watched it, getting his breath back, and then half-leapt, half-scrambled to the big white bulge near the base of the mast.

A shadow passed over him, and he rolled to one side as the mast nicked a furrow in the hull. As it passed he followed it, grabbed at the nerve knot, and pulled himself forward.

His fingers sought for the right spot. He found it.

The shell stopped its frenzied rush through the wavetops, hitting the water again with a slap that jarred Dom's teeth. The sail wavered uncertainly.

Dom continued stroking until the creature was soothed and then stood up.

It didn't count unless you stood up. The best dagon fishers could ride a shell with their toes. How he had envied them – and how carefully he had watched from the family barge on feast days, when the fishermen came in two or three hundred abreast on their half-tame shells with See-Why setting, a bright purple star, into the sea. Some of the younger men danced on their shells, spinning and leaping and juggling torches and all the time keeping the shell under perfect control.

Kneeling in front of the nerve knot he guided the big semi-vegetable back through the twisting waterways of the marsh, through acres of sea lilies and past floating reed islands. On several of them blue flamingoes hissed at him and stalked imperiously away.

Occasionally he glanced up and northwards, searching for tell-tale specks in the air. Korodore would find him eventually, but Dom was pretty certain that he wouldn't pick him up straight away. He'd probably keep him under benevolent observation for a few hours because, after all, Korodore had been young once. Even Korodore. Whereas Grandmother gave the impression that she had been born aged eighty.

Besides, Korodore would bear in mind that tomorrow Dom would be Chairman and legally his boss. Dom doubted if that would influence him one jot. Old Korodore relished duty if it came sternly . . .

He smiled proudly as the shell cut smoothly through the quiet water. At least the fishermen would not be able to call him a blackhand, even if he wasn't quite a fully fledged greenhand. That last initiation of the dagon fishermen could only be got out in the deeps, on a moonlit night, when the dagons rose out of the deep with their razor-sharp shells agape.

The shell bumped against the reed bed and Dom leapt lightly ashore, leaving it drifting in the little lagoon.

Joker's Tower, which had been dominating the western sky, looked up before him. He hurried forward.

See-Why had risen and bathed the slim pyramid in pink light. The mist had left the reed beds round the base but the apex, five miles above the sea, was lost in perpetual cloud. Dom pushed his way through the dry reeds until he was within half a metre of the smooth, milk-white wall.

He reached out gingerly.

Hrsh-Hgn had once, realizing vaguely that interminable lectures on planetary economics might not be palatable fare for a boy, smiled and switched off the faxboard. He had fetched his copy of Sub-Lunar's *Galactic Chronicles* and told Dom about the Jokers.

'Name the races classed as Human under the Humanity Act,' he began.

'Phnobes, men, drosks and the First Sirian Bank,' Dom rattled off. 'Also Class Five robots by Sub-Clause One may apply for Human status.'

'Yess. And the other racess?'

12

Dom ticked them off on his fingers. 'Creapii are Super-Human, Class Four robots are sub-human, sundogs are unclassified.'

'Yess?'

'The other races I'm not sure about,' admitted Dom. 'The Jovians and the rest. You never taught me anything about them.'

'It iss not necessary. They are so alien, you undersstand. We share no common ground. Things humanity considers universal among self-aware races – a sense of identity, for example – are merely products of a temperate bipedal evolution. But all the fifty-two races so far discovered arose in the last five million standard years.'

'You told me about that yesterday,' said Dom, 'Sub-Lunar's Theory of Galactic Sapience.'

Then the phnobe had told him about the Jokers. The Creapii had found the first Joker tower and, all else having failed to open it, had dropped a live nigrocavernal matrix on it. The tower was later found to be intact. Three neighbouring stellar systems had been wrecked, however.

The phnobes never discovered a Joker tower: they had always known of one. The tower of Phnobis, rising from the sea into the perpetual cloud cover, was the cause and basis of the planet-wide Frss-Gnhs religion – literally, Pillar of the Universe.

Earth-human colonists had found seven, one

of them floating in the asteroid belt of the Old Sol system. That was when the Joker Institute was set up.

The young races of men, Creapii, phnobe and drosk found themselves watching one another in awe across a galaxy littered with the memories of a race that had died before human time began. And out of that awe arose the legends of Jokers World, the glittering goal that was to taunt adventurers and fools and treasure hunters across the light years . . .

Dom touched the tower. There was the faintest tingle, a sudden stab of pain. He leapt back, frantically rubbing life back into his frozen fingers. The coldness of the towers was always greatest at noon, when they drank in heat, yet grew icy.

Dom set off round the tower, feeling the cold reaching out towards him. Looking up he thought he saw the air within a foot of the smooth walls darken, as if light was just a gas and was being sucked in by the spire. It wasn't logical, but the idea had a certain artistic appeal.

Towards noon a security flyer glittered briefly on the western horizon, heading south. Dom stepped sideways into a clump of reeds . . . And wondered what he was doing in the marsh. Freedom, that was it. The last day of real freedom. His last chance to see Widdershins without a security guard standing on either side of him and a score of more subtle protections all

14

round. He had planned it, down to squashing Korodore's ubiquitous robot insects that spied on him – always for his own protection – in his bedroom.

And now he'd have to go home and face Grandmother. He was beginning to feel just a little foolish. He wondered what he had expected from the tower: some feeling of cosmic awe, probably, a sense of the deeps of Time. Certainly not this sinister, insidious sensation of being watched. It was just like being at home.

He turned back.

There was a hiss of superheated air as something passed his face and struck the tower. Where it hit the frozen wall the heat blossomed into a flower of ice crystals.

Dom dived instinctively, rolled over and over and was up and running. A second blast passed him and a dry seed head in front of him exploded into a shower of sparks.

He stifled the urge to look round. Korodore had schooled him unmercifully in assassination drill. Knowing who was the assassin was small reward for being assassinated. Korodore said, 'The price of curiosity is a terminal experience.'

At the edge of the lagoon Dom gathered himself and dived. As he hit the water the third blast seared across his chest.

Great bells rang, far out to sea or maybe in his head. The cool greenness was soothing, and the bubbles . . .

*   *   *

Dom awoke. With an inculcated instinct he kept his eyes closed and tentatively explored his environment.

He was lying on the mixture of sand, ooze, dry reed stems and snail shells that passed for soil on most of Widdershins. He was in shade, and the thunder of surf was very near. And the soil rocked, gently, to the beat of the waves. The air smelled and tasted of salt, mingled with marsh ooze, reed pollen and . . . something else. It was dank and musty, and very familiar.

Something was sitting a few inches away. Dom opened one eye a fraction and saw a small creature watching him intently. Its dumpy body was covered in pink hair which sprouted from a scaly hide. A snout was a bad compromise between a beak and a prehensile nose. It had three pairs of legs, no two exactly alike. It was almost a Widdershins legend.

Behind Dom someone lit a fire. He tried to sit up and it felt as though a red-hot bar had been laid across his chest.

'O juvindo may psutivi,' said a gentle voice.

A face out of a nightmare appeared above him. The skin was grey and hung in folds under eyes four times the proper size in which small irises stared out like beads in milk. Great flat ears were turned towards Dom. The musty smell was over-powering. The face was set off by a pair of large sungoggles.

16

The phnobe was trying to speak Janglic. Dom summoned his resources and answered him in jaw-breaking phnobic.

'A sscholar,' said the phnobe, dryly. 'My name is Fff-Shs. And you are Chairman Sabalos.'

'Not till tomorrow,' moaned Dom. He winced as the pain came again.

'Ah. Yess. Do not on any account make ssudden movementss. I have treated the burn. It iss superficial.'

The phnobe stood up and walked out of Dom's vision. The small creature still watched him intently.

Dom turned his head slowly. He was lying in a small clearing in the centre of one of the floating islands that thronged the marsh rhines. It was moving slowly and, remarkably, against the wind. From somewhere below the reed mat came the occasional deep pulse of an antique deuterium motor.

A coarse woven net was slung across the clearing, hiding it effectively from airborne eyes. With the motor and the ancillary mechanisms that must be hidden under the thick reed mat, the little island would not hold its secret long against even unsophisticated search equipment. But there were several hundred thousand islands in the marsh. Who could search them all?

A conclusion began to form in Dom's mind.

The phnobe passed in front of him and he saw he was holding a double-bladed tshuri knife

17

lightly, tossing it thoughtfully from hand to hand. Dom was mother-naked, except where dry salt rimed his black skin.

The phnobe was embarrassed by his presence. Occasionally he stopped juggling with the knife and stared at him intently.

They both heard the distant swish-swish of a flyer. The phnobe dived sideways, flipped back a section of reed and killed the island's speed, then on the rebound flung himself down by Dom with the knife pressed against his throat.

'Not to utter a sound,' he said.

They lay still until the flyer had faded into the distance.

The phnobe was a pilac smuggler. The dagon fishermen under licence from the Board of Widdershins rode out by the hundred when the big bivalves rose up from the deep, to snatch the pearls of nacreous pilac by the light of the moon. They used lifelines, leather body armour and elaborate back-up procedures – like the factory float which included a hospital where a missing hand was merely a minor mishap and even death not always fatal.

There were other fishers. They traded safety for an odd conception of excitement and accepted as the price of an illegal fortune the complete lack of any opportunity to spend it. By nature they worked alone and were highly skilled. What they snatched from the sea was theirs alone, including death. Occasionally the Board launched a campaign against them and made half-hearted attempts to stop the pilac being smuggled off-world. Captured smugglers were not killed now – that would certainly be against the One Commandment – but it occured to Dom that to those of their nature the alternative punishment was far worse than the death they courted nightly. So the smuggler would kill him.

The phnobe stood up, still holding the knife by the heavier, forward-facing blade.

'Why am I here?' asked Dom, meekly. 'The last I remember . . . '

'You were floating among the lilies sso peacefully, with a stripper burn across your chest. The ssecurity has been out ssince dawn. It seemed they were searching, for a criminal maybe, so I am jusst a little curiouss and pick you up.'

'Thank you,' said Dom, easing himself into a sitting position.

The smuggler shrugged, a strangely expressive gesture in a high-shouldered bony body.

'How far are we from the Tower?'

'I found you forty kilometres from the Sky Pillar. We have travelled maybe two kilometres ssince.'

'Forty! But someone shot at me at the Tower.'

'Maybe you swim well for a drowned man.'

Dom lifted himself gradually to his feet, his eyes on the twisting knife.

'Do you gather much pilac?'

19

'Eighteen kilos in the last twenty-eight years,' said the phnobe, watching the sky absently. Despite himself, Dom did a quick calculation.

'You must be very skilful.'

'Many times I die. On other time lines. Maybe this universe is my chance in a million and the other thousands of selves are dead. What is skill then?'

The knife continued its brief flights from hand to hand. Overhead the sun shone like a gong. Dom felt dizzy and was briefly sick but managed to stay upright, waiting for his chance.

The phnobe blinked.

'I seek an omen,' he said.

'What for?'

'To see, you understand, if I am to kill you.'

A flock of blue flamingoes flapped slowly overhead. Dom gasped for air and readied himself.

The knife was thrown faster than he could follow it. It flashed once, high in the air. A flamingo dipped out of the flock as if coming in to land, and crashed heavily among the reeds. The tension in the air snapped like a finely drawn wire.

Ignoring Dom, the smuggler loped across to it, drew his knife from its breast and began to pluck it. He paused after a minute and glanced up sharply, pointing with the knife.

'A word of advice. Do not ever again even think of a heroic leap at any person holding a tshuri knife. You have about you the air of one with many lives to wasste. Maybe therefore you rissk your life easily. But foolish gestures towards a knife end sadly.'

Dom let the tension flow out of him, aware that a fraught moment had passed and gone.

'Besides,' the smuggler went on, 'doesn't gratitude count for anything? Soon we will eat. Then we will talk, maybe.'

'There's a lot I want to know,' said Dom. 'Who shot at . . .'

'Tssh! Questions that can't be answered, why ask them? But do not rule out *bater*.'

'Bater?'

The phnobe looked up.

'You haven't heard of probability math? You, and tomorrow you become Chairman of the Board of Widdershinss and heir to riches untold? Then first we will talk, and then we will eat.'

See-Why hung in the mists that had crept out of the marsh. The island sailed dripping through the clammy curtain, leaving a mist-wake that writhed fantastically over the suddenly sinister marsh.

Fff-Shs came out of the woven hut at one end of the island and pointed into the whiteness.

'The radar says your flyer iss hardly more

21

than a hundred metres thataway. Sso I leave you here.'

They shook hands solemnly. Dom turned and walked down to the water's edge, then turned again as the phnobe hurried after him. He held the little rat-creature, which had spent most of the journey asleep round his neck.

'Tomorrow, maybe, there will be great ceremoniess?'

Dom sighed. 'Yes, I'm afraid there will.'

'And giftss, maybe? That iss the procedure?'

'Yes. But Grandmother says that most will be from those who seek favours. Anyway, they'll be returned.'

'I sseek no favours, nor will you return thiss small gift,' said the phnobe, holding out the struggling creature. 'Take him. You know what he iss?'

'A swamp ig,' nodded Dom. 'He's one of the bearers on our planetary crest, along with the blue flamingo. But the zoo says there's only about three hundred on the planet, I can't . . .'

'This little one has dogged my footsteps these last four months. He'll come with you. I feel he will desert me soon anyway.'

The ig jumped from the phnobe's arm and settled around Dom's neck, where it re-placed its tail in its mouth and began to snore. Dom smiled, and the smuggler answered with a brief mucus grimace.

'I call him my luck,' said the phnobe. 'It's an

indulgence, maybe.' He glanced up at Widder-shins's one bloated moon, rising in the south.

'Tonight will be a good night for hunting,' he said, and in two strides had disappeared into the thickening mists.

Dom opened his mouth to speak, then stood silent for a moment.

He turned and dived into the warm evening sea.

The heavy hull of a security flyer rocked in the swell beside his own craft. A figure appeared on the flat deck as he hauled himself aboard.

Dom found himself looking first at the crosswires of a molecule stripper and then at the embarrassed face of a young security man.

'Chel! I'm sorry, sir, I didn't realize . . .'

'You've found me. Good for you,' said Dom coldly. 'Now I'm going home.'

'I've got orders, er, to take you back,' said the guard. Dom ignored him and stepped aboard his own craft. The guard swallowed, glanced at the stripper and then at Dom, and hurried into the control bubble. By the time he had reached the radio, Dom's flyer was a hundred metres away, bouncing lightly from wavetop to wavetop before gliding up and over the sea.

*   *   *

Extract from *2001 and All That: an Anecdotal History of Space-Travelling Man*, by Charles Sub-Lunar (Fghs-Hrs & Calligna, Terra Novae)

'Mention should be made of Widdershins and of the Sabalos family, since the two are practically synonymous. Widdershins, a mild world consisting largely of water and very little else, is one of the two planets of CY Aquirii. Its climate is pleasant though damp, its food a monotonous variation on the theme of fish, its people intelligent, hardy and – due to the high ultraviolet content of the sunlight – universally black and bald.

'The planet was settled in the Year of the Questing Monkey (A.S. 675) by a small party of earth-humans and a smaller colony of phnobes and there, perhaps, pan-Human relations are better than on any other world.

'John Sabalos – the first of his dynasty – built himself a house by the Wiggly River, looking over the sea towards Great Creaking Marsh. His only skill was luck. He discovered in the giant floating bivalves that dwelt in the deep waters a metre-wide pearl made up largely of crude pilac, which turned out to be one of the growing number of death-immunity drugs. But pilac was found to be without many of the unfortunate drawbacks of many of the other twenty-six. It became the foundation of the family fortunes. John I extended his house, planted an orchard of cherry trees, became the first Chairman when

Widdershins adopted Rule by Board of Directors, and died aged 301.

'His son, John, is considered a wastrel. One example of his wastefulness suffices: he bought a shipload of rare fruits from Third Eye. Most were rotten on arrival. One mould was a strange green slime. By an unlikely combination of circumstances it was found to have curious regenerative properties. Within a year, just when dagon fishing was becoming almost impossible because of the high injury rate among the fishermen, it became a mark of manhood to have at least one limb with the peculiar greenish tint of the cell-duplicating googoo.

'John II bought the Cheops pyramid from the Tsion subcommittee of the Board of Earth and had it lifted in one piece at an area of waste ground north of his home domes. When he made an offer for Luna, to replace Widdershins' smaller but still serviceable moon, his young daughter Joan I packed him off to a mansion on the other side of the planet and took over as Managing Director. In her the Sabalos fortunes, hitherto dependent on a smiling fate, found a champion. They doubled within a year. A strict Sadhimist, she executed many reforms including the passage of the Humanity Laws.

'Her son – she found time for a brief contract with a cousin – was John III, who became a brilliant probability mathematician in those early, exciting days of the art. It has been suggested that this was a peaceful escape from his mother and his wife Vian, a well-connected Earth noblewoman to whom he had been contracted in order to strengthen ties with Earth. He disappeared in strange circumstances just prior to the birth of his second child, the Dom Sabalos of legend. It is understood that he met with some kind of accident in the planet-wide marshes.

'A body of myth surrounds the young Dom. Many stories relating to him are obviously apocryphal. For example, it is said that on the very date of his investiture as Chairman of the Planetary Board, he . . .'

The stars were out as Dom reached the jetty which stretched from the home domes far out into the artificial harbour where the feral windshells were kept.

Lamps were burning. Some of the early-duty fishermen were already preparing the shells for the night's fishing; one old woman was deep-frying King cockles on a charcoal stove, and a tinny radio lying on the boards was playing, quite unheeded, an old Earth tune with the refrain, 'Your Feet's too Big'.

Dom tied up at the jetty alongside the great silent bulk of a hospital float, and scrambled up the ladder.

As he walked towards the domes he was aware of the silence. It spread out from him like a wake, from man to man. Heads rose in the lamplight and froze, watching him intently. Even the old woman lifted the pan from the stove and glanced up. There was something acute about the look in her eyes.

Dom heard one sound as he slowly climbed the steps towards the main Sabalos dome. Someone started to say: 'Not like his father, then, whatever they—' and was nudged into silence.

A Class Three robot stood by the door, armed with an antiquated sonic. It whirred into life as he approached and assumed a defiant stance.

'Halt – who goes there? Enemy or Friend of Earth?' it croaked, its somewhat corroded voice-box slurring the edges of the traditional Sadhimist challenge.

'FOE, of course,' said Dom, resisting the urge to give the wrong answer. He had done it once to see what would happen. The blast had left him temporarily deaf and the resonance had demolished a warehouse. Grandmother, who seldom smiled, had laughed quite a lot and then tanned his hide to make sure the lesson was doubly learned.

'Pass, FOE,' said the guard. As he passed, the communicator on its chest glowed into life.

'Okay,' said Korodore, 'Dom, one day you will tell me how you got out without tripping an alarm.'

'It took some studying.'

'Step closer to the scanner. I see. That scar is new.'

'Someone shot at me out in the marsh. I'm all right.'

Korodore's reply came slowly, under admirable control.

'Who?'

'Chel, how should I know? Anyway, it was hours ago. I . . . uh . . .'

'You will come inside, and in ten minutes you will come to my office and you will tell me the events of today in detail so minute you will be amazed. Do you understand?'

Dom looked up defiantly, and bit his lip.

'Yes, sir,' he said.

'Okay. And just maybe I will not get sent to scrape barnacles off a raft with my teeth and you will not get confined to dome for a month.' Korodore's voice softened marginally. 'What's that thing round your neck? It looks familiar.'

'It's a swamp ig.'

'Rare, aren't they?'

Dom glanced up at the planetary coat of arms over the door, where a blue flamingo and a bad representation of a swamp ig supported a Sadhimist logo on an azure field. Under it, incised deeply into the stone – far more deeply in fact than was necessary – was the One Commandment.

'I used to know a smuggler who had one of those,' Korodore went on. 'There are one or two odd legends about them. I expect you know, of course. I guess it's okay to bring it in.'

The communicator darkened. The robot stood aside.

Dom skirted the main living quarters. There was an uproar coming from the kitchens where preparations were being made for tomorrow's banquet. He slipped in quietly, snatched a plate of kelp entrées from the table nearest the door, and ducked back into the corridor. A phnobic curseword followed him, but that was all, and he wandered on down to the corridor until it petered out in a maze of storerooms and pantries.

A small courtyard had been roofed over with smoked plastic that made it gloomy even under a See-Why noon, and the plastic itself was set with thin pipes that sprayed a constant fine mist.

In the middle of the yard a rath had been built of reeds. An attempt to grow fungi had been made on the patch of ground surrounding it. Dom pulled aside the drenched door-curtain and stooped inside.

Hrsh-Hgn was sitting in a shallow bath of tepid water, reading a cube by the light of a fish-oil lamp. He waved one double-jointed hand at Dom and swivelled one eye towards him.

'Glad you're here. Lissten to thiss: "A rock outcrop twenty kilometres south of Rampa, Third Eye, appearss to reveal fossil strata relating not to the passt but to the future, which . . ."'

The phnobe stopped reading and carefully placed the cube on the floor. He looked first at Dom's expression, then at the scar, and finally at the ig which was still twined round his neck.

'You're acting,' said Dom. 'You are doing it very well, but you *are* acting. You're certainly acting better than Korodore and the men on the jetty.'

'We are naturally glad to see you ssafely back.'

'You all look as though I've returned from the dead.'

The phnobe blinked.

'Hrsh, tomorrow I shall be Chairman of the Board. It doesn't mean much—'

'It iss a very honourable position.'

'—It doesn't mean much because all the power, the real power, belongs to Grandmother. But I think the Chairman is entitled to know one or two things. Like, for example, why haven't you ever told me about probability math? And what happened to – how did my father die? I've heard fishermen say it was out there on Old Creaky.'

In the silence that followed the ig awoke and began scratching itself violently.

'Come on,' said Dom, 'you're my tutor.'

'I will tell you after the ceremony tomorrow, it iss late now. Then all will be explained.'

Dom stood up. 'Will I ever trust you again, though? Chel, Hrsh, it's important. And you're still acting.'

'Oh, yess? And what emotion am I trying to conceal?'

Dom stared at him. 'Uh . . . terror, I think. And – uh – pity. Yes. Pity. And you're terrified.'

The curtain swung to behind him. Hrsh-Hgn waited until his footsteps had died away, and reached out to the communicator. Korodore answered.

'Well?'

'He hass been to ssee me. I almosst told him! My lord, he wass reading me! How can we let thiss thing happen?'

'We don't. We will try and prevent it, of course. With all our power. But it will happen, or seventy years of probability math go down the hole.'

Hrsh-Hgn said, 'Someone hass been telling him about probability math, and he assked me about his father. If he assks again, I warn you, for pity's ssake I will tell him.'

'Will you?'

The phnobe looked down and fell silent.

Out to sea the dagon rose by the score, in response to their ancient instincts. The catch was unusually large, which the fishermen decided was an omen, if only they could decide which way fate's finger pointed. They found, too – when the last ripple had died away towards dawn – a small reed island, empty, half swamped, drifting aimlessly over the deeps.

2

Korodore strolled silently along the empty corridor, which was lit faintly by the first glow of dawn.

He was thickset and, as a sly gesture, heredity had given him a round cheerful face so that he looked like an amiable pork-butcher. But there were advantages to that, and no butcher – certainly not of pork – walked by instinct from shadow to shadow.

A door opened soundlessly and he turned along a short side corridor and into a large round room.

A peat fire was collapsing soundlessly into a pile of white ash in the central hearth. The rest of the room was sparsely furnished: a narrow bed, a table and chair made of sections of dagon shell, a wardrobe and a Sadhimist logo on sheet copper on one curving wall comprised its main geographical points.

There were one or two signs of Directorship, a large rolled map of the equatorial regions, an open filing cabinet, and a Galactic Standard clock on top of it.

But it was the trappings of probability math that clashed heavily with the strict simplicity of the room. Korodore's eye followed a trail of Reformed Tarot cards across the room to where the bulk of the pack, crystal faces now bland, lay against the wall where it had been thrown. A vaguely disturbing visual array on a portable computer glowed on another wall. Charcoal glowed faintly in a tiny brazier on the shell table, and the air was acrid with the fumes of – Korodore sniffed the curious Sinistral incense. So Joan had taken refuge in being a cool-head . . .

Joan I looked up from the table, where a large black book lay open.

'Couldn't you sleep either?' she said.

Korodore rubbed his nose diffidently.

'As you know, madam, security officers never sleep.'

'Yes . . . I know.' She shook her head. 'It was a figure of speech, is all. There's some coffee by the fire.'

He poured her a cup, and slowly began to pick up the cards. She eyed him carefully as he moved soundlessly across the room.

'I've been looking at the equations again,' she said. 'There's no change. My son's calculation was correct. Of course, I knew. They've been checked enough times. Even Sub-Lunar looked at them. Dom will be killed today, at noon. They won't let him live.'

She waited. 'Well?' she said.

'You mean, how do I feel as the security officer in charge? You mean, what are my reactions to the knowledge that whatever precautions I may take my charge will still be murdered? I have none, madam. I will still work as though I was in ignorance. Besides,' he added, dropping the pack on the table, 'I cannot believe it. Not quite. You could say my reaction is hope.'

'It'll happen.'

'I can't pretend to understand probability math. But if the universe is so ordered, so – *immutable* – that the future can be told from a handful of numbers, then why need we go on living?'

Joan stood up, crossed to the wardrobe, and took out of it a waist-length white wig.

'It's obvious you do not understand p-math, then,' she said. 'We go on because to live is still better than to die. That has always been the choice of Humanity, even when we thought the future was a cauldron of possibilities.'

She combed out the wig. 'We cannot be certain how he will die,' she continued. 'You or I, perhaps, may be the ones the Institute chooses to—'

Korodore spun round. 'I have checked us all by deep-reach, RGD—'

'Oh, Korodore! I'm sorry. But you have

such a touching faith in cause and effect! Don't you know that in an infinite Totality all universes will happen? There is a universe somewhere where at this moment you will turn into a—'

'Such things are said, madam,' he muttered.

'You disapprove of me,' she said, and pouted.

He raised his eyes to the gold century disc on her forehead and smiled thinly.

'Now, you are too old, madam, to try wiles of that kind. But I do disapprove. This meddling is not a good thing. It stinks of magic, witchcraft.'

'I haven't studied the pre-Sadhimist religions in any great depth, Korodore.'

'All right, madam. *What happens if Dom doesn't die?*'

'It's unthinkable. This is the datum universe – he'll die. In a sense, the whole universe depends on the fact. If he didn't die, perhaps he'd discover the Jokers World and that could be terrible.'

'And if he doesn't?'

Joan adjusted the wig and opened the window looking out over the sea. The fishing fleet was coming in with the tide, lit by the hanging pinpoint of Widdershins' blue sun. On the horizon the light glinted sharply off the Tower in the marshes.

'It's too hot to sleep,' she said. 'I'll finish this, and then I'll go down to the jetty.'

'Mystic law of the universe?' asked Korodore, as she reopened the book.

'They are the household accounts, sir,' she said sharply. 'A great comfort in times of trial.'

She wondered why she had never dismissed the man as security chief, and the answers queued up in her mind, ranging from his proven efficiency to the mitigating circumstance that he was Earth-born. Perhaps there were many other reasons.

As he turned to go she called him back.

'With regard to your question about Dom,' she said, 'in all humility, p-math is a young art. I doubt if there is anyone adept enough to know. Even the Institute doesn't know everything.'

'Dom might. His tutor says he is showing a disconcerting insight. Oh, I don't question your reasoning. If it is inevitable, perhaps it is better he shouldn't know. You can see he is the type the Institute hunts down.'

'You see, we can't answer all the questions.'

He shrugged. 'Perhaps you are asking the wrong questions.'

PROBABILITY MATH:

'As with the first Theory of Relativity and the Sadhimist One Commandment, so the nine equations of probability math provide an example of a deceptively simple spark initiating a great explosion of social change.

' "Probability math predicts the future." So says the half-educated man. A thousand years ago he would have mouthed "E equals MC squared" and believed he had encompassed the soaring castle of mathematical imagination . . .

'Probability math arises from the premise that we dwell in a truly infinite totality, space and time without limit, worlds without end – a creation so vast that what we are pleased to call our cause-and-effect datum Universe is a mere circle of candlelight. In such a totality we can only echo the words of Quixote: *All things are possible* . . .'

'. . . vindicated with the predicted discovery of the Internal Planets of Protostar Five. Then humanity could be sure – even from this tiny grain of proof. On either "side" were ranged the alternate Universes, uncounted millions differing perhaps by the orbit of an electron. Further, the difference must be greater – until in the looming shadows on the edge of imagination came the universes that had never known time, stars, space or rationality. What p-math did was quantify the possible timelines of our datum universe. It did much more than that, however. Perhaps it brought back the essence of science from the days when it was half an art, when Creation was seen as a marvellous, carefully regulated clock – with all parts harmonizing to make the whole . . .'

'. . . As Sub-Lunar pointed out in those early

years, p-math depended on a certain innate mental agility. Many superb practitioners were also incurably insane, possibly because of that very fact. Leaving aside that very special sub-group to which Sub-Lunar himself belonged – I say no more – the rest were usually highly educated and, in a word, lucky. (Luck being a function of the p-math talent, of course.) Many of them worked for the Joker Institute.

'Such a streak ran through the Sabalos family of Widdershins. For those of you who do not know the world, it is . . .'

'. . . just before the birth of his son and his own assassination in the marshes, John III predicted that the boy would die also on the day of his investiture as Chairman of the Planetary Board. The chance of this *not* happening was so remote as to make a billion-to-one long shot appear a fifty-fifty bet. Yes? I'm sorry. Perhaps I should explain.

'Suppose p-math had not been discovered. Now, on Earth there was a creature called a horse. Long ago it was realized that if a number of these animals were raced over a set distance one must surely prove faster than the others, and from this there was . . .'

'. . . back to the subject in hand. One anomaly in p-math concerned the Jokers, those semi-mythical beings who had left artefacts strewn around half the galaxy. Solid artefacts, indeed, most of them gigantic. According to probability math, the builders of these latter-day tourist attractions had never, ever existed . . .'

His Furness Dr CrAarg+458°, in an informal lecture to students at Dis university, A.S. 5,201

Dom woke early, and spent a long time staring at the familiar ceiling paintings of his dome. They had been done by his great-grandfather, in gaudy blues and greens, and depicted a trio of overmuscled fishermen battling an enraged dagon. That was a slander on the dagons, Dom knew: they lacked a nervous system and it was doubtful if they ever thought. They just reacted.

The little swamp ig was sitting in the hand-basin. It had managed to turn on one of the taps with its disconcertingly human forepaws, and was enjoying the trickle of water. When it saw he was awake it made a noise like a fingernail being dragged across glass. The smuggler had said it was a sign of happiness.

'Intelligent little thing, aren't you?' said Dom, switching off the warm air field and swinging himself off the bed.

He saw the clothes laid out neatly on the stand, and bit his lip. The swamp ig, a neatly healed scar on his chest and a few painful memories of his interview with Korodore were all that remained of yesterday.

Planetary Chairman. He'd own 3 per cent of

the pilac industry, but on Sadhimist terms, and if you were a Sadhimist and rich you worked heavily to obscure the fact. He'd preside over innumerable committee meetings, and once a year would give the traditional annual report at the traditional Annual General Meeting. And that would be written for him. Hrsh-Hgn had made it clear, many times. A Chairman was as necessary to a Board planet as the zero was in mathematics, but being a zero had big disadvantages . . .

Mathematics. There was something about mathematics he should remember. Well, it'd come. He washed and struggled into the thick grey suit, and selected a short wig of golden fibres.

There was a polite knock at the door.

'All right,' said Dom.

The door burst open and Keja ran into the room and hugged him. She was laughing and crying at the same time. For an embarrassing moment he was suffocated by the silks of her dress, and then his sister stood back and looked at him.

'Well, Mr Chairman,' she said. Then she kissed him. He disentangled himself as tactfully as he could.

'I'm not actually Chairman yet,' he began.

'Oh fie! What's a few hours? You don't seem very pleased to see me, Dom,' she added, reproachfully.

41

'Honestly I am, Ke. Things have just been a bit hectic lately.'

'I heard. Smugglers and so forth. Exciting?'

Dom thought about it. 'No,' he said. 'More, well, strange in a way.'

Keja swept the dome with her eyes. It was cluttered with Dom's things: an old Brendikin analyser, a bench littered with shells, a hologram of the Jokers Tower, and memory cubes on every flat surface.

'How the old place has changed,' she said, wrinkling her nose. She pirouetted in front of the tall mirror. 'Do I look like a married woman, Dom?'

'I don't know. What's Ptarmigan like?' He remembered the contractual ceremony two months before, and a vague impression of a very large fierce old man.

'He's kind,' said Keja. 'And rich, of course. Not so rich as us, but he sort of *flaunts* it more. His children haven't really taken to me yet. You should come on an official visit, Dom – Laoth's so hot and *dry*. That reminds me, I've brought you a present.'

She tiptoed to the door and returned with a servant robot, which carried a small box.

'He's a Class Five. One of our best,' she said proudly.

'A robot?' said Dom, who had been looking expectantly at the box.

'Strictly speaking, he's a humanoid. Completely alive, merely mechanical. Do you like him?'

'Very much!' Dom walked up to the tall metallic figure and prodded the broad chest. The robot glanced down at him.

'I wonder what makes us build inefficiently shaped human robots instead of nice stream-lined machines?'

'Pride, sir,' said the robot.

'Hey, that's not bad. What's your name?'

'I understand it is Isaac, sir.'

Dom scratched his head. The home domes swarmed with robots, mostly kind but stupid Class Threes whom Dom remembered from earliest childhood as sad, boring voices with firm, child-minding hands. His mother, who seldom left her own dome, disliked them generally and did her own cooking. She said they were morons, and not a bit like the real things from Laoth. He was at a loss.

'Uh, can you be a bit more informal, Isaac?'

'Sure thing, boss.'

'I can see you two are going to get along fine, trying to out-think each other,' said Keja. 'Now I've got to go. And Grandmother says you've got to go down to the main dome, Dom. For the Working Breakfast.'

Dom sighed. 'I've had about twenty lectures about it from Hrsh-Hgn in the last few days.'

Keja stopped dead.

'What's that thing?' she cried, pointing to the basin.

Dom lifted the damp creature out by the scruff of its neck.

'It's a swamp ig. I call him Ig. I was – I found – I, er . . .' He blinked nervously. 'I *think* I found him in the marshes yesterday. I – er – things seem a little confused.'

She looked at him, and Dom saw the concern in her eyes.

'It's all right,' he mumbled. 'It's just the excitement.'

'I guess so,' Keja said, and looked down at Ig. 'Anyway, he's so ugly!'

'Excuse me, madam, sir, but he is an it,' boomed the robot. 'Hermaphrodite. Oviparous. Semi-poikothermic. I have been supplied with a complete program on Widdershins lifeforms, sir. Chief. Right on.'

'Well, don't blame me if you catch a zoonose,' said Keja, and flounced out of the dome. Dom looked at Isaac.

'Zoonose?'

'Disease communicable to humans. No chance, buster.' Isaac strode up to Dom and held out the box. The boy dropped his pet, who began to sniff at the robot's foot, and opened it.

'It's the certificate of warranty, workshop manual and deed of property,' said Isaac. Dom looked at them blankly.

'Do you mean I have to *own* you?'

'Body and hypothetical supernatural append-age, boss,' said the robot hurriedly, stepping backwards when Dom held the box towards him.

'Oh no, chief. You've got to. I don't approve of self-ownership.'

'Chel, that's what most humans fought for for three thousand years!'

'But we robots know exactly why we were created, boss. No striving to find the innermost secrets of our creation. No problem.'

'Don't you want to be free?'

'What? And have God blame the Universe on me? Shouldn't you go down to the main dome now?'

Dom whistled, and Ig scrambled up and went to sleep round his neck. He glared up at the robot and strode out of the dome.

Tradition decreed the Working Breakfast be taken alone by the Chairman on the day of his investiture. As he walked along the deserted corridors Dom had the comfortably familiar feeling he was being watched. Old Korodore had the place seeded with pinheads and robot insects – it was dome gossip that he even ran security checks on himself.

The main dome was half clear plastic, facing out across the orchards, the lagoon and marshes and finally, a thin line on the horizon, the Jokers Tower with a wisp of white cloud streaming

45

from its tip like a banner. Dom stared at it for a few seconds, trying to hold an elusive memory.

A pile of presents – he was, after all, half a whole Widdershins year old – were heaped around the long table. Two robots-in-waiting stood on either side of the single place setting.

Dom had planned the meal time and again. In the end he had chosen the menu that had been eaten by every Chairman of Widdershins. It was a famous meal. According to the Newer Testament, it was the same meal that Sadhim Himself ate when he became Lord of Earth – a quarter-loaf of brown bread, a strip of salt-dried fish, an apple and a glass of water.

There were some slight differences. The flour for Dom's loaf had been freighted in from Third Eye. The fish was truly Widdershin, but the salt had been mined on Terra Novae. The apple was from the Earth's Avalon, the water melted from a particle of comet. In all, the meal cost about two thousand standards. Some kinds of simplicity cost more than others.

Korodore, a true-born Terra Novaean, which meant food concentrates, watched Dom eat with a slight feeling of nausea. The camera was in a metal mosquito, high in the dome. He thumbed a switch, and the screen faded in a view from a mechanical shrew in the branches of a tree on the edge of the west lawn. Most of the guests had already arrived, and were mingled around the long buffet table.

46

At least half of them were phnobes, many of them from the *buruku* colonies around Tau City. Korodore recognized the diplomats – they were tall, dark alpha-males, carrying sunshades. The less exalted, who were more acclimatized to the light, stood in small, silent groups around the lawn. Korodore switched from pinhead to pinhead until he located Hrsh-Hgn, reading a memory cube in the shade of a balloon tree. The Stoics, probably.

Behind Korodore the darkness of the big security room glowed here and there as the other security officers watched. Only Korodore knew that under the horticultural dome by the north lawn was another, smaller security room checking on this one. And occasionally he switched to his own private circuit and watched the officers there. And, hidden by him in a place the exact location of which he had scrubbed from his mind, was a small biocomputer. He had programmed it carefully. It watched him.

He turned back to the guests. Here and there a big gold egg now showed in the crowd – the Creapii ambassadors. Experience suggested that there was no risk in them. They seldom meddled in the affairs of worlds where water liquefied.

One was holding a dish of silicate-salt hors d'oeuvres in a single armoured tentacle. Occasionally it held on to the complicated airlock on its circumference. It was chatting to Joan I,

who stood majestic in the black memory velvet
and purple tabard of a Sadhimist Dame-Priestess
in the negative aspect of Nocticula-Hecate. Lady
of Night and Death, thought Korodore. It was
not a tactful choice.

She smiled at the Creapii and turned to face
the hidden camera, raising one hand. Korodore
reached out and tipped a switch.

'How goes it?' Joan asked. Korodore watched
fascinated – she had a remarkable talent for sub-
vocalizing.

'He is breakfasting. We have treble-checked
the food and everything else.'

'Has he shown any effects from yesterday?'

Korodore paused. 'No. While he slept I used a
brain scrubber on him. I—'

'How dare you!'

'It will keep yesterday's memories in a state
of flux for a few hours. Would you prefer him
to learn the truth? He would, had I not done so
– even if he had to brow-beat it out of Hrsh-
Hgn.'

'You should have asked me!'

Korodore sighed, and picked up a memory
cube on the console. 'I'm sorry, madam, but you
have a security rating now of only 99.087 per
cent. I checked. Probably it's only deep Freudian
impulses – but from now on I am afraid I must
run this show.

'Like I said, madam, I'm not inclined to accept
probability math. You may, if you like.'

He switched off. She stood rigid for a moment, trying to contact him, then turned and began to talk brightly to a tall diplomat from the Board of Earth.

Korodore turned his attention to the main hall. Dom wasn't there. His heart stopped until he realized that the boy had also moved out of one camera's range to look at his presents.

Dom opened the first package and drew out a pair of gravity sandals, glistening under their thin coat of oil. The tag said: 'From your God-father. Come up and orbit me some time. It gets damn lonely.'

Dom grinned and buckled them on. For a hectic few minutes he bobbed and swooped among the struts of the dome, gliding to an unsteady halt six inches above the floor. He felt that the sandals would probably be the climax – most of the other presents would be much less interesting.

From Hrsh-Hgn came a fat rectangle. Dom unwrapped a memory cube and ran his finger over the index face. The cube lit up, the title page standing out in white letters a few centimetres above the surface and revealing: 'The Glass Castles: A History of Joker Studies, by Dr Hrsh-Hgn. Dedicated to Chairman Dominickdaniel Sabalos of Widdershins.'

In smaller letters Dom read: 'Number One in a

limited edition of one (1) imprinted on Third Eye saffron-silica.'

'A high honour, indeed,' said Isaac. Dom nodded, and thumbed the cube at random to read: '. . . mystery of the galaxy. As Sub-Lunar has said, to the imaginative mind they form part of galactic mythology: the Glass Castles at the back of the Galactic North Wind. These towers, built before the oldest of the official Human races had discovered the uses of stone, are memorials to a race which—'

Dom laid the cube down slowly and opened the present from Korodore.

'That looks dangerous,' said Isaac.

Dom wielded the memory sword carefully, staring up at the almost invisible blur as it changed under his touch from sword to knife, from knife to gun.

'Hm,' said Dom. 'They use swords on Earth and Terra Novae, don't they? And on Laoth, too?'

'Yes, with metal blades. They're more ceremonial and satisfying than guns. But that thing is made to kill people with. Not that I'm putting it down, boss.'

Dom grinned. 'You're mighty uppity for a robot, aren't you? In the old days you'd have been dismantled by the mob.'

'In the old days robots were considered to be non-living, chief.'

Joan's present was a simple black Sadhimist

athame against the time when he should be admitted to membership of a ceremonial klatch, while from his mother he received the deeds of one of her personal estates on Earth. It was far too generous, and typical of Lady Vian on those occasions when she remembered Dom.

There were other presents from the minor directors and heads of subcommittees, most of them expensive – far too expensive to be allowed to keep, even if Joan would permit it. But Dom looked wistfully at the deeds of a robot horse, presented by Hugagan of Planetary Relations. Isaac peered over his shoulder and sneered audibly.

'Lunar manufacture,' he said. 'All right, I suppose, but not a patch on the ones we make on Laoth. They *live*.'

Dom glanced at him.

'I shall have to visit Laoth,' he said.

'The jewel of the universe, take it from me.'

Dom laughed and made sure that Ig had a good purchase on his shoulder. Then he thumbed the control ring and the sandals lifted him up, through the dust-laden beams that filled the dome, and out over the sea.

He spiralled low over the lagoon, where Lady Vian's little tame windshells grazed, and felt Ig scramble around his neck. He glanced backwards and saw the little animal was riding him comfortably, pointed snout sniffing the wind.

Below him he watched the shells cease their

grazing and swing into a pattern so that, prow to stern, they formed a circle. Vian spent hours drumming simple tricks into their microscopic minds.

Something stirred restlessly at the back of his memory, but he dismissed it carelessly and sought altitude.

He burst through the balloon trees ringing the lawn, bursting the fruits recklessly, and braked a bare inch above the grass.

Joan I strode across the lawn to meet him, and kissed him with rather more tenderness than usual. He looked into her grey eyes.

'Well, grandson, and how do you feel this day?'

'I feel on top of the world, madam, thank you. But I must say you look rather tired.' She's acting like a cool-head, he thought – why is she so worried?

She smiled wanly. 'It is always hard when one's descendants make their way out into the world. Now you must come and meet people.'

Lady Vian had walked slowly up, her face hidden in a heavy grey veil. She extended a white hand. Dom knelt and kissed it.

'So,' she said, 'enter the master of the world. Who is your ferrous friend?'

'Isaac, my lady,' said Dom. 'An uppity robot who doesn't want his freedom.'

'But of course,' said Vian, 'we are all of us in chains, even if they be only of chance and entropy. Have not the Jokers put even the stars in chains?'

'You have a fine grasp of essentials,' said Isaac, bowing.

'And you are presumptuous, robot. But I thank you. Dom, I wish you would donate that swamp creature to a museum or a zoo or something. It is so *animal.*'

Ig scratched himself and sniffed – then gave a long drawn-out hiss. Dom looked over his mother's shoulder and caught the eye of a tall man in a long blue cloak, who wore a heavy gold collar at his neck. The man's face was creased with laughter lines, and he winked at Dom and gestured upward with his glass. Dom followed his gaze and saw a flock of flamingoes wheeling high over the domes. For a moment they formed a circle. Then, with long slow wingbeats, they flew out to sea.

Korodore sat back and breathed deeply. Short of poisoning the air – and a filter haze surrounded the lawn – the only way someone could attack Dom now was with bare hand or tentacle. At least, they could try, before concealed strippers separated them from their component molecules.

There remained the official progress through Tau City. Dom would walk while the others rode, and would wear nothing but the lead and iron chain of office and seven invisible shields of various types, incorporated in the links. Most of the human worlds and one or two alien ones would have the route bugged, of course, and several had bribed Korodore. He . . .

. . . leant forward. Someone had walked into the field of one pinhead and was looking at him. Korodore had an uneasy certainty that the man was laughing. He looked like a man who had laughed all his life.

Korodore thumbed through the guest list. Blue cloak, tall . . . the man was a minor official at the Board of Earth's agency in Tau City, newly appointed . . .

The man in the screen had lifted one foot so that he was balancing on his right leg.

'Madern, get a focus on the guy in the blue cloak. No, better – Gralle, can you get a beam on him?'

'Got it, Ko. Shall I take him out?'

Korodore considered. Earth was still powerful. Standing on one leg wasn't a killing matter *per se*.

'Hold it.'

The figure had extended its left arm, pointing the first and fourth fingers directly towards, it appeared, the security room. He had closed one eye and was sighting along the extended arm like a weapon.

Let's see how you look without an optic nerve, thought Korodore.

The explosion knocked him sideways. He landed at the crouch, stripper levelled in a reflex

54

action, and dived again as a second explosion and the beginning of a scream marked the weapon control console's transformation into a plume of incandescence.

The guests applauded politely. Dom, at his grandmother's nod, rose a few metres above the ground and said: 'I thank you all. And I ask that the spirit of holy Sadhim and the small gods of all races give me – give me—' He stopped.

A low boom echoed from the home domes.

Dom stared, and heard again in his inner ear the thin crack of a stripper shot in the transparent air around Jokers Tower. Images flooded into his mind, with fragments of speech that joined and became coherent, and the memory of the hot pain and the cool green relief of the swamp water . . .

A dot in the air grew rapidly. He heard his mother cry out, a long way off.

Korodore dived with his clothes smouldering. Raw blisters were his hands, blood was his face.

He landed heavily by Dom and shouted incoherently at him. Dom nodded, lost in a dream.

The man in the blue robe stepped lightly towards them, and took his theatrical stance. Ig shrilled.

Korodore lurched forward, raised the stripper

in both hands, and gave a growl and dropped its smoking butt. In the same motion he flung himself towards the outstretched arm.

The ball of non-light spun up above the blackened lawn and the landscape twisted. See-Why was a bright sun. In the painfully light sky it showed now as a darker speck.

3

'Understanding is the first step towards control. We now understand probability.

'If we control it every man will be a magician. Let us then hope that this will not come to pass. For our universe is a fragile house of atoms, held together by the weak mortar of cause and effect. One magician would be two too many.'

Charles Sub-Lunar, *Cry Continuum*.

'The fish swims – vsss!
The bird flies – rsss!
The fungi-squirrel run – gsrss!
The wheel turns and
All is one.

'I must scream yet I have no mouth.
I must run yet I have no feet.
I must die yet I have no life.
The wheel turns and
All is one.'

Funeral song of the Deep Rocky region,
Five Islands, Phnobis.

*   *   *

The sound of the sea. Breathe? But he could not breathe.

It came and went like the surf. It was only a sound, but it carried strange harmonies – warmth, and softness.

Dom floated somewhere on the breathing sea.

A man appeared, dressed in the old brown robes of a Sadhimist adept garbed for the ceremonies of Hogswatchnight. The face was familiar. It was his own.

'Don't be so damn silly. I am your father.'

'Hullo, Dad. Is it really you?'

John Sabalos gestured aimlessly. 'No, I am an extension of your own deep mind. Hasn't Hrsh-Hgn taught you anything? Chel! Down all the stars, boy, you should be dead. So much for probability math, therefore.'

'Dad, what's happening to me?'

The familiar face faded. 'I don't know – it's your dream,' was left hanging in the air.

Hrsh-Hgn appeared, standing in front of the familiar faxboard.

'In an infinite universe all things are possible, including the possibility that the universe does not exisssst,' he purred. 'Expand this theory, with diagramsss—'

Dom heard himself say: 'That is not a theory. That is a mere hypothesis.'

'Ahh, beware of paradox!' The phnobe shook a

finger. 'For once you have a paradox let loose in the universe you have a poiyt.'

'Poiyt?'

'And let uss consider . . .'

Isaac appeared, doing a soft-shoe shuffle through the mists.

'Goodness, are robots allowed in this dream? Or do they have to sit in the second-class dream at the back? Now here's the plot, boss, see, really you are the hereditary chairman of Earth itself but because of a palace coup you were sent here—'

'No,' said Dom firmly. That wasn't right.

'No, you have this wild talent which is the result of generations of careful breeding and all you have to do is give the word and hordes will—'

'Not me. Try the Infinity next door.'

'No, well, the universe doesn't really exist – we can't hide this from you – except in your imagination, and so this secret organization called the Knights of Infinity, they—'

'Try some other universe, robot.'

'Well, okay, if you want it straight from the shoulder, you are not important at all but you happen to have this magic bracelet which was made by the God of the Universe and He wants it back and you have got to get together a few trusted friends, such as me, and travel many a weary light year to the searing fires of Rigel and—'

'Uhuh.'

'I was only trying to cheer you up, chief.' The robot shed a tear of mercury. 'We Freudian extensions of personality have feelings too, you know!'

Dom.

'Who are you?'

Dom, can you hear me?

'I can hear you. What are you?'

Dom, if you can't hear me, what can you see?

See?

He sensed a light *above*, tinted with green.

Good, Dom, you are in psuedodeath. You do not know what that means. We need your earnest co-operation. We need access to your self-memory. Will you perform these exercises? Good. Now we want you to form a mental picture of yourself. We will show you how . . .

A long time passed. Before Dom's mind swam himself, a perfect copy. It danced, and sang, and flexed embarrassing muscles. Then the voice made him go through it all again. And again.

Understanding was allowed into his mind. The voice was that of a googoo tank operator. Or, rather, a series of them.

He had seen the men of the hospital rafts after a hard night with the dagons, grinning foolishly under the pallid nutrient bath as they flexed the muscles of their new green-grown limbs. Googoo was one invention Widdershins hugged to itself. The surgeons said that if no more of a body was left than that tiny sliver of brain they called the mommet, a new body could be . . .

60

No!

Dom thought it again. He could sense the tank man's panic. Dom started to think questions. Darkness fell swiftly, and was replaced by the green light and no desire to ask questions at all. A new voice said:

Think coherently. You must breathe. We have some more building to do. Think of something, say it in your mind, now.

Unbidden, the Green Paternoster floated up through Dom's consciousness, the last words he would say before climbing into his cot as a child, after ending the night prayer with 'God bless the household robots'.

He galloped through it. It was senseless gibberish now, the centuries had twisted the words, but it still had power.

'Green Paternoster, Sadhim was my foster, He saved me under the poisoned tree, He was made of flesh and blood to send me my right food, mine right food and air, too . . .'

Good.

' . . . that I might be a FOE, and stop at two, To read in that sweet book which the great gods shoop . . . '

Good.

Dom plunged on recklessly, tasting the words: ' . . . open, open, save me, Dead, Dead Chel Sea, Halve the population roster and say the Green prayer PATER NOSTER!'

In the silence the tank man said: 'Dom, you

now have vocal cords. You are breathing. You have built yourself a mouth. There is something you must want to do.'

Dom screamed.

He examined himself in the full-length mirror. Everything was there, and in full working order. The tank, working from his body memory, had duplicated nails, teeth, DNA patterns and even healed the scar on his chest. Dom rubbed the place bitterly, remembering the flight in the marsh.

Isaac creaked across the room and handed him his clothes. He dressed himself slowly.

There was one alteration. Before he had been jet black and decently hairless, the result both of See-Why's healthy ultra-violet and the tannin injections. Now he had hair to the waist and, like the rest of him, it had a greenish tint.

The bouncy little Creapii doctor in charge of the hospital tanks had explained it carefully, with a rare grasp of colloquial Janglic. But then Creapii could so easily assume the mannerisms of other races.

'It's called googoo. Of course, I needn't tell *you* that. I used to go out on the hospital rafts once, but we've come a long way from those primitive limb replacement tanks.

'Anyway, Mr Chairman, it is alive in its own right. It is in fact a highly complex organism under your control. I can guarantee that it matches your body almost on the atomic level. It will have certain advantages, of course – your heat tolerance, for example . . . ah, yes, at your age I'm not surprised you should ask. Yes, your children will be human in every respect—' and the doctor made a surprisingly apt dirty joke. 'But be careful of misunderstandings. It is now *you*, not some alien slime. The colour? The state of the art, I'm afraid . . . come back in, oh, ten years and I guarantee that we can turn out a body with not even a trace of green. As for the hair, well, absence of hair is not yet a generic characteristic of a Widdershins. I'm sorry, at the moment it's a warts-and-all process.

'Before you go, Mr Chairman, I would like to show you the hospital. I'm sure the staff would like to meet you, uh, unofficially. As for myself, I am proud to shake you by the manipulatory appendage.'

Dom fastened his choker collar and turned round.

'How do I look?'

'Pale green, boss,' said Isaac soberly. He indicated a small plastic case.

'There are some body cosmetics here, boss. Your mother sent them.'

Dom turned again and ran his pale green fingers over his face. The googoo had tried to follow body pigmentation as far as possible, but even so he looked as if he had been on a copper-rich diet for a year. He had watched himself on the newscasts while he was recuperating. The fishermen were already fiercely proud of a Chairman who was completely green, and didn't seem to mind that it was not as a result of prowess on the hunting sea. But his mother's unspoken comment was that it would offend offworld dignitaries.

'Beng take them!' he said out loud. 'What do they matter. Anyway, green is a holy colour.'

Outside the little hospital six security guards stood to attention as Dom walked out, followed by Isaac and, at a discreet distance, some of the hospital staff.

Hrsh-Hgn waited beside them. He was holding a high-velocity molecule stripper, and looking sheepish.

'It suits you,' said Dom.

'I am a pacifist, ass befits a philosopher, and thiss is barbaric.'

They boarded the Chairman's barge, which was joined by five flyers as soon as it was airborne.

Dom stared unseeing at the seascape.

'Who is replacing Korodore?' he asked after a while.

'Darven Samhedi, from Laoth.'

'A – a good man.' But still, it took more than efficiency to be security man on Widdershins. 'Will the phnobes take to him?'

'He is rumoured to have shown shape-hatred. We will ssee.' Hrsh-Hgn looked down at Dom. 'You were fond of Korodore.'

'No. He didn't encourage friendship, but . . . well, he was always there, wasn't he?'

'Indeed.'

Dom turned in his seat and looked at Isaac.

'And if you say one sarcastic word, robot . . .'

'No, chief. It crossed my mind that Lord Korodore was somewhat over-enamoured of miniature cameras but that was his job. He was a regular guy. I mourn.'

Four months ago, thought Dom, someone killed him and tried to kill me.

I am going to find out why.

A light drizzle was blowing when the squadron landed at the second Sabalos home, a small walled dome near the administrative centre of Tau City. Even Lady Vian came out to meet him, bundled in a heavy cloak, and looking slightly happier for being in a city. Tau was not overwhelmingly cosmospolitan, though a sight more so than the home domes.

'That is not a becoming colour,' were her first words.

They dined in the small hall. Down the table Samhedi and the senior members of the household eavesdropped respectfully. Joan, after a polite enquiry about the hospital, was silent.

Vian looked across at her son. 'Why don't you try those body cosmetics?'

Dom caught the eye of a security man standing against the wall. He had one green hand and a green patch extended all down one cheek and into the colour of his uniform. The man saw him and winked.

'I prefer it this way.'

'Perverse vanity,' said Joan. 'But still, I agree. A piebald grandson I could not bear, but at least he is a uniform colour.'

She pushed her plate aside and added: 'Besides, green is a holy—'

'Green is the colour of chlorophyll on Earth, certainly,' said Vian, 'but here the vegetation is blue.'

Joan glanced up quickly at the Sadhim logo inscribed on the ceiling and then gazed at her daughter-in-law, her eyes narrowing. Dom watched them interestedly – too much so, for Joan sensed him and folded her napkin deliberately. She stood up.

'It is time,' she said, 'for our evening devotions. Dom, I will see you in my office in one hour's time. And we will talk.'

4

Dom entered. His grandmother glanced up, and nodded towards a chair. The air was musty with incense.

The large white-painted room was completely empty except for the small desk and two chairs and the little standard thurible and altar in one corner, though Joan had a way of filling up empty spaces with her presence.

In foot-high letters along the facing wall the ubiquitous One Commandment glared down on them.

Joan closed her account book and began to play with a white-hilted knife.

'In a few days it'll be Soul Cake Friday, and also the Eve of Small Gods,' she said. 'Have you given much thought to joining a klatch?'

'Not much,' said Dom, who hadn't thought at all about his religious future.

'Scares you, eh?'

'Since you put it like that, yes,' said Dom. 'It's a rather final choice. Sometimes I'm not sure

Sadhimism has all the answers, you see.'

'You're right, of course. But it does ask the right questions.' She paused for an instant, as if listening to a voice that Dom could not hear.

'Is it necessary?' prompted Dom.

'The klatch? No. But a bit of ritual never did anyone any harm, and of course it is expected of you.'

'There is one thing I'd like to get clear,' said Dom.

'Go ahead.'

'Grandmother, why are you so nervous?'

She laid down the knife and sighed.

'There are times, Dom, when you raise in me the overwhelming desire to bust you one on the snoot. Of course I'm nervous. What do you expect?' She sat back. 'Well, shall I explain, or will you ask questions?'

'I'd like to know the story. I think I've got some kind of right. A lot has been happening to me lately, and I kind of get the impression that everyone knows all about it except me.'

Joan stood up, and walked over to the altar. She hoisted herself onto it and sat swinging her legs in an oddly girlish way.

'Your father – my son – was one of the two best probability mathematicians the galaxy has ever seen. You have found out about probability math, I gather. It's been around for about five hundred years. John refined it. He postulated the Pothole Effect, and when that was proved,

68

p-math went from a toy to a tool. We could take a minute section of the continuum – a human being, for example – and predict its future in this universe.

'John did this for you. You were the first person ever quantified in this way. It took him seven months, and how we wish we knew how he managed it, because even the Bank can't quantify a person in less than a year with any degree of accuracy. Your father had genius, at least when it came to p-math. He . . . wasn't quite so good at human relationships, though.'

She shot an interrogative glance at Dom, but he did not rise to the bait. She went on: 'He was killed in the marshes, you know.'

'I know.'

John Sabalos looked out over the sparkling marshes, towards the distant tower. It was a fine day. He surveyed his emotions analytically, and realized he felt content. He smiled to himself, and drew another memory cube towards him and slotted it in the recorder.

'And therefore,' he said, 'I will make this final prediction concerning my future son. He will die on his half-year birthday, as the long year is measured on Widdershins, which will be the day he is invested as Planetary Chairman. The means: some form of energy discharge.'

He switched off for a few seconds while he collected his thoughts, and then began: 'The assassin: I cannot tell. Don't think I haven't tried to find out. All I can see is a gap in the flow of the equations, a gap, maybe, in the shape of a man. If so, he is a man around whom the continuum flows like water round a rock. I know that he will escape. I can sense him outlined by your actions like – damn, another simile – a vacuum made of shadow. I think he works for the Joker Institute, and they are making a desperate attempt to kill my son.'

He paused, and glanced down at his equation. It was polished, perfect, like a slab of agate. It had an intrinsic beauty.

The distant glint of the Tower drew his gaze again. He glanced up. Not the right time, not yet. Another hour . . .

'And now, Dom, as you stand there torn between shock and astonishment, what do you see? Does your grandmother have that tight-lipped, determined look she wears at times of stress? How was the party, anyway?

'Dom, you are my son, but as you are perhaps learning, I have many sons – untold millions. Have, I say, but "had" I mean. For in those billions of universes that hedge us about on every side, they are dead as I predicted. You, who are flesh and blood, are also that one chance that lies a long trek behind the decimal point. That chance that I am wrong. But a student of probability soon realizes that by its nature the billion-to-one chance crops up nine times out of ten, and that the greatest odds boil down to a double-sided statement: it will happen, or it will not.

'I have studied you, and the billion-to-one universe in which you now stand. It left the main-sequence universe at the point of your non-death. Universes are like the stars which some of them contain. Most follow the well-beaten path. But some, by the twist of a photon, career down strange histories which end in supernovae or impossible holes in space. Rogue universes now, crack under the stress of paradox or – what?

'I will try to give you some help, because you will need it. Your assassin came from your present universe, can you understand that? He wanted to prevent you discovering something that will make your chance-in-a-billion universe the greatest in all the alternate creations. But I've an inkling that whatever saved you from death came from your universe, too. I've seen a lot in your universe but how can I tell you because, believe me, Dom, if I did the paradox burden would split your universe at the seams.'

He laid down the recorder and wandered idly into his outer office. The secretary robot clicked into life.

'If anyone calls I am going out to the Tower. I, uh, shouldn't be long.'

71

'Yes, Mr Chairman.'

'You'll find a cube on my desk. Please send it to Her Managing Directorship.'

'Certainly.'

John Sabalos closed the door and went back to his desk. He was still wearing his black and brown robes from the Hogswatch celebrations of the night before. He hadn't slept, but he felt exhilarated. It was false, of course. Knowing the future wasn't the same thing as controlling it. It just felt like it. He picked up the recorder.

'This I can say, however. Three things. You will discover the Jokers World, if you look in the right directions. Your life will be in danger. And, thirdly . . . look up in the corner of the room! *Run for your life!*'

He switched off, and laid the cube on his desk.

Somewhere outside, over towards the east lawn, someone was playing the phnobic *chlong* zither, badly. John stepped outside. The clatter of Joan's old electric computer floated up from the kitchen domes, which meant she was processing the eighth-year household accounts.

He breathed deeply. Something was adding a third dimension to his senses, etching the external world in high relief. With a probability adept's skill he located the cause. The world was like wine, because this was his last day in the world. The last of the wine. And, they would kill him before he discovered Jokers World. Dom should be luckier.

His personal flyer bobbed in the swell, down by the long jetty.

The door slid to. With a light tread, he set off, quelling the wild elation that ran through him, because death was a serious matter.

His father's voice stopped and the cube projection stopped. Dom shot a glance upwards.

Something small glittered in the air, like a mote of metallic dust. He heard Joan's voice, every word as crisp as frosty air.

'Samhedi, there's another one in here. Be ready.'

'What is it?' asked Dom. The fleck appeared to have grown.

'A collapsed proton. Does that help you?'

'Sure. Like in a matrix engine.'

'Something like that. By the look of it it's already ingested its own atom. What you can see is angular light effect. It's being controlled.'

The first thing that Dom realized was that both of them were standing like statues. The second was . . .

'I have seen that before.'

'It was the gravity whirlpool that got you before, though. Take one step now and it'll be a bullet with teeth. Ever been sucked through a hole one micron across?'

'Uhuh.'

'I'm sorry, that was tactless. If Samhedi doesn't get here soon you won't have to bother about that, though.'

'Asphyxiation? It'll suck the air out of the room.' She nodded.

Samhedi's voice came from the wall grille.

'When I say so, please to lie flat on the floor, keeping away from the approximate centre of the room . . . now!'

Dom caught a glimpse of a flying silver ball the size of a grape before he hit the floor.

When he rolled over it was floating a metre above his head. There was an odd sensation of heat along his spine. They had caught it in a matrix field. It was still sucking up air like a miniature tornado. Presently it drifted out through the wall, leaving a hole with its edges twisted into high-stress shapes. He could hear shouts outside, and the whine of the matrix generator.

He helped Joan to her feet.

'You seem to have it all figured out,' he said.

'It was a sensible precaution. After your – your party, it was days before we figured out how to get rid of the damn thing. It was your robot who came up with the answer.'

'You couldn't put it on a ship because it would eat its way through the floor . . . Isaac? What did he suggest?'

They watched through the hole. On the lawn outside, Samhedi's equipment was clustered around the baby black hole. The silvery sheen had disappeared now. It appeared as a point in space that wrenched at the optic nerves, and the men working around it had to hang on against the wind that was driving into nowhere.

Three of them manhandled a tall cylinder until it was standing upright under the thing. The cylinder was thick with matrix coils.

'This should be quite impressive,' said Joan.

'I'm getting the idea, I think,' said Dom. 'The bottom of the tube is sealed, the matrix field stops it touching the edges, the air rushes in at the top . . .'

Samhedi bellowed an order against the gale. The thing – it looked like an eye now, a malevolent one staring straight at Dom – dipped into the cylinder.

There was an explosion.

It was the cylinder, reaching Mach One a mile overhead. It sucked itself on towards the stars.

'Neat,' said Dom. 'Suppose it hits the sun? No, you'd have a ship up there. Then what?'

'Seal it up and dump it in deep space. Isaac suggested finding a genuine black hole and dumping it there. That sounds like an invitation to blow up the universe, though, so Hrsh-Hgn suggested accelerating it to about half as light as it was. It'd accelerate, he believes, on interstellar hydrogen.'

'And end up drilling a hole in someone's planet on the other side of creation,' said Dom. He was trying to smile.

His grandmother reached out and took his shoulder.

'You're not doing badly at all, Dom.'

'You neither, Grandmother.'

'Just because I am reasonably adept at disassociation. You won't see me when I choose to turn off.'

Dom shuddered despite himself. He had been with friends when they turned off after DA trips. It was a discipline only taught within the Sadhimist klatches. A man could go for days, weeks, without being affected by his emotions. One or two had told him it was a great sensation – there was a feeling of icy intellectual power, an ability to face problems shorn of the deceptive roccoco of feelings. Cool-heads, they were called. And then you turned off, and the backlash hit you, and you were glad to have an emotional friend around to unroll you with a crowbar and put you to bed – preferably with a bullet.

'How long have you been cool?' he asked.

'Since dinner. And for most of the last four months. But that doesn't matter. You seem to have mastered the technique, anyway. Without drugs, too.'

'Don't you believe it.'

'One thing I'll ask you to believe is that I never heard that second part of that cube before. He was talking to you. He did it—'

'He did it for the million-to-one chance. Oh, there's lots of ways. If he'd foreseen all this, he could have put a simple time delay into the cube. Lots of ways,' he said reassuringly.

'And what will you do now?' Dom tensed at the undertone in her voice.

'It seems I've got to discover the Jokers World. Half the history cubes say it never could have existed.'

'I can't let you,' said Joan.

'I'll be safe until I discover it. You heard the prediction.'

'Your father could have made another mistake. There might be a million-to-one chance, another one. Dom, someone is trying to kill you! That was the third attempt!'

Dom backed away as she walked forward.

'But the first time I dived into the marsh and I turned up forty kilometres away. The second time something saved enough of me from that thing – someone's trying to save me, too! I want to find out who, and why.'

He took another step back and let the door slide across. Then he turned and ran.

'SADHIMISM: the pantheistic/conservation religion founded in cold blood by Arte Sadhim (q.v.), the ruler of Earth from 2001–12. Contemporary documents suggest that he devised the dogmas, beliefs and rituals of Sadhimism in a day and a night, incorporating gobbets wrenched wholesale from druidism, the marginally surviving witchcraft practices, voodoo and the Survival Handbook for Spaceship Earth. As a religion it worked well and achieved its purpose, which was solely to impress environmental thinking deeply on human minds, and then developed a life of its own and became greater than its creator. Sadhim himself was ritually murdered by a breakaway sect called the Little Flowers of the Left-hand Path on the eve of Good Friday – the Night of the Long Athames . . .'

Charles Sub-Lunar: *Religions of a Hundred Worlds.*

Dom lay on his bed, reading a long rambling letter from Keja. She was glad to hear that he was better; life on Laoth was quite pleasant, and there would be a state visit to Earth soon, and she had seen snow for the first time – and enclosed a refrigerated cube in which several snowflakes were preserved – and dear Ptarmigan had built her a garden that Dom really ought to see . . .

Isaac slipped in on well-oiled feet.

'Well?'

'There's guards all over the place, boss. I

can't find that gecky frog anywh—'

'That's shape-hatred talk, Isaac.'

'Sorry, chief. The cook says he's left the domes and moved down to the *buruku*.'

Dom buckled on his grav sandals. 'We're going to fetch him. He's the only one round here that knows more than three facts about the Jokers. And then I kind of think we're going to look for the Jokers World.'

The robot nodded impassively.

'Well? Aren't you going to ask why?'

'Up to you, boss.'

'It's just as well. It seems I've got to fulfil a prediction. I've been pretty bad at fulfilling them lately. I think I will find one or two answers on the way. You know about the third attempt to kill me?'

'Oh yes, and all the others.'

Dom froze. He looked up from stuffing clothing into a back-pouch and spoke slowly.

'How many others?'

Isaac hummed. 'A total of seven. There was the poisoned food in hospital, the meteorite that just missed the power plant, two attacks on the flyer that brought you here. And another artificial black hole. That turned up in the hospital. You were still in the tank then.'

'They all failed—'

'By luck only, chief. The hospital food – I think you didn't eat it, but one of the cooks did. The meteorite—'

79

'Odd attempts. Inefficient, too.' He thought for a moment, and then packed the memory sword that Korodore had given him. As he turned, his eye caught the pink cube resting on the cubecase. Hrsh-Hgn's Joker thesis. He packed it.

'I'm not safe here, that's for sure. We leave now, while it's still night.'

'If you try and fly you'll fry. Samhedi's got the force screens up around the walls. We could try walking out. You'll have to order me to use necessary force, though.'

'Right,' said Dom.

'In full, please. If the fuzz get me afterwards, it'll all be down on my recorders. Can't disassemble a robot for obeying orders: Eleventh Law of Robotics, Clause C, As Amended,' said the robot firmly.

'Then get me out of here, using no more force than is necessary.'

The robot walked over to the door and called in the security man who was standing guard down the corridor. Then he pole-axed him.

'Not bad,' he said. 'Enough to stun but not enough to shatter. Let's split, boss.'

The *buruku* was built on the outskirts of the city, where the dry land sloped towards the marsh. It looked like a field of mushrooms under a grey dome. Each mushroom was a reed-woven *rath*, some of them several times larger than a

80

human geodome. The grey dome was the low-degree force screen, just powerful enough to keep the atmosphere within damp and still. It was polarized too, so that the light that filtered through was dim and subterranean. Inside the air was warm, clammy and smelled of decay. Dom felt that if he breathed deeply horrible moulds would sprout in his lungs. It was what 10,000 phnobes called home.

Towards the centre of the colony the raths huddled together in a fungal township riddled with alleyways and sprouting several distressingly organic-looking towers and civic buildings. Shops were still open, though it was well past midnight; they mostly sold badly dried fungi, fish or second-hand cubes. From some of the larger raths, bulbous as fermenting pumpkins, came snatches of haunting *chlong* music. And all around Dom phnobes filled the streets.

In a purely human environment a solitary phnobe looked either pathetic or disgusting, from its goggled eyes to the slap of its damp feet on the floor. In the rath they loomed like ghosts, self-assured and frightening. Most of the alpha-males carried long double-bladed daggers, and any visitor with a concealed inclination towards shape-hatred ended up walking with his back pressed firmly against a comfortingly solid wall.

At one point they had to press into the crowd as a wickerwork delivery truck trundled by.

It stank: it was powered by a ceramic engine fuelled with fish oil.

And the air was filled with hissing, a susurration like the wind, the sound of phnobic speech. Dom enjoyed the *buruku*. The phnobes had a way of life divorced entirely from the carefully stylized penury of a Sadhimist ruling family.

Dom found Hrsh-Hgn seated in a communal *jasca*, playing tstame. He glanced up at the two of them, and waved them into silence.

Dom sat down on the stone seat and waited patiently. Hrsh-Hgn's opponent was a young alpha-male, who looked at Dom disinterestedly before turning back to the board.

The tstame men were crude and badly co-ordinated, which was to be expected from a public set. Even so, they were being directed across the squares with a gawky grace.

Red's pawns had dug a defensive trench across one corner of the board. White had tried the same tactic, but had stopped work and the pawns were clustered around one of Red's knights, who was haranguing them. As Dom watched, Red's Sacerdote-Shaman brought his mitrepike down on the kill-button of White's Accountant, and in the ensuing mêlée managed to get several pawns through the crossfire from the Rooks. The King made a brave attempt to run for it but was brought down by a flying tackle from the leading pawn.

Hrsh-Hgn's opponent removed his helmet

and made a grudgingly complimentary comment in phnobic before loping away. Dom's tutor turned.

'I want you to help me find Jokers World,' said Dom.

He explained.

The phnobe listened politely. At one point he said: 'I'd be interessted to know how you survived a black hole that removed Korodore.'

'Yes, and Ig.'

'But no, that is not sso . . .' He reached down beside him and picked up a wicker cage. Inside, Ig fizzled.

'I found him in the busshess at the edge of the lawn. He was badly sshaken. He must have left your sshoulder somehow.'

'And you looked after him – that's surprising, for you.'

Hrsh-Hgn shrugged. 'No one elsse would. The fisshermen are supersstitious of them. They ssay they are the ssouls of dead comrades.'

The swamp creature looped itself around Dom's neck.

'Are you coming with me . . . us?'

'Yess, I think sso. I accept *bater*.'

'I never did find out what that word meant.'

'It refers to the inexorable processsesss of what you humans are pleased to call Fate. Where did you think of starting? Don't look so blank.'

'It's just that I expected a lecture on my duties

as Chairman. As my tutor you were hot on the subject, I seem to remember.'

The phnobe smiled, switched his headset on and turned to the board. The tstame mannikins stood up, ranged themselves into two neat rows, and marched down a flight of steps that appeared in one of the neutral squares, carrying the temporarily disabled.

'The point doess not arise now,' he said. 'Ass a mere frog' – he looked sharply at Isaac – 'I suggesst you follow the path predicted. Bessides, ass a Joker student of ssome repute, and an amateur probability mathematician to boot, I feel intrigued. Tell me, are you embarking upon thiss because it hass been seen to happen in the future, or has it been seen to happen in the future because you are following the prediction now?'

'I don't know,' said Dom. 'But I know where there's a ship—'

'Mr Chairman!'

Impressions crowded in on him. The low-ceilinged room had gone quiet, suddenly, like the switching off of a music cube, leaving the sort of silence that is even louder and hangs in the air like fog. The players bent over the tstame tables did not move, but now they seemed tense.

The *chlong* trio stopped playing. Ig whined.

Samhedi stood in the doorway, flanked by two minor security men. And they were armed.

Dom remembered Korodore's advice, one day when the dead man was feeling expansive, that only the foolhardy or unimaginative carried projectile weapons into a *buruku*. Korodore had in fact hefted a regulation double-bladed knife, and then diffidently, on the rare occasions he went in.

'We have come to escort you home, Mr Chairman.'

Dom strode towards him and said politely, too politely: 'You were number two on Terra Novae, weren't you?'

'I was.'

'Who told you to carry stunners into a *buruku*?'

Samhedi swallowed, and glanced sidelong at the guards. The room seemed to sprout ears.

'Your predecessor would not have done such a thing. You might just have precipitated an interracial incident. Now unbuckle those things and throw them on the floor.'

'I have orders to see you safely home—' began Samhedi.

'From my grandmother? She has no authority. What law am I breaking? But you're breaking phnobic custom—'

He had driven the man too far. Samhedi growled.

'What gecky customs do these frogs have, anyway?'

He said it in bad phnobic. One by one the

phnobes stood up, tshuri knives glinting in the deep gloom.

The alpha-male that had played tstame with Hrsh-Hgn loped up to Samhedi and threw his knife into the floor between them. Samhedi looked at Dom.

'It's a challenge,' said Dom.

'Suits me.' The security man raised his stunner until it was level with the phnobe's face. The phnobe blinked impassively.

Samhedi fired. It was a low-intensity beam, just enough to stun. The phnobe fell backwards like a sapling.

'And that's my—'

Dom had disappeared. A knife took the stunner and two fingers from the man's hand. He gaped, and looked up at the ring of blank, large-eyed faces . . .

Isaac helped the two of them through a small rear window as the noise in the *jasca* rose suddenly. They darted across the road just ahead of two flatcars laden with security men.

'The stupid geck,' said Dom. 'Oh Chel, the stupid geck!'

'Intelligence is humanity's prime ssurvival trait, therefore it iss as well that those who don't sshow it be weeded out,' said Hrsh-Hgn, philosophically.

'Where to now, chief?' said Isaac. 'Round here

it's beginning to look like Whole Erse on Slain Patrick's Eve.'

'Great-great-grandfather was occasionally less than honest in his business dealings. There's a private yacht at the spacefield. It's there for use if any high-ranking Sabalos feels the need for a – a—'

'An impromptu vacation?' suggested Hrsh-Hgn.

5

The universe was divided into two parts, separated by a five centimetre shell of mono-molecular steel. On the inner side was the interior of the luxury yacht *One Jump Ahead*, superbly outfitted for one passenger but badly cramped for three, one of whom was metal and another was smelling of swamp water.

On the other side was the rest of the universe, composed almost entirely of nothing with a trace of hydrogen. There were also the inhabited planets of Human-Creapii space.

There was Terra Novae, metal-rich and dynamically technological. Third Eye, forested from tundra to mangrove swamps, where the wind sang eerily in the trees and the humans were more alien even than phnobes, and talked with their minds and eyes. On Eggplant the vegetarians were ferocious, and had to be. On the drosk's world of Quaducquakucckuaqueke-kecqac visiting humans picked uneasily at the horribly familiar food and were thankful that drosks were too well mannered to do more than look hungrily at guests. There was Laoth, where the only living things were human beings – yet birds flew and the brooks were full of fish . . .

On every world hot enough to boil water one of the sub-races of Creapii clustered. In the deceptive emptiness of space swam the sundogs and the race called The Pod. And there was The First Sirian Bank . . .

'Sixteen,' said Isaac.

'This is a distrustful universe in which we live, certainly,' said Hrsh-Hgn.

Ig, with the ease of one who had lived in zero-g all his life, floated around a bulkhead with another struggling body in his mouth. It looked vaguely like a grasshopper, and had in fact quite a sophisticated copy of an insect brain – but rather better than insect ears.

Dom turned from the viewscreen. 'Old Korodore really had this ship bugged,' he said. 'Look for pinheads, too.'

From orbit Widdershins was grey-blue and big, studded with strips of cloud. The dawn terminator was nudging Tau City. A grey cloud hung over it.

The drive cabin was small and apparently full of elbows. Isaac sat hunched up in the pilot couch. He looked up.

'I have your grandmother on the line, chief. Are you in?'

'Does she sound angry?'

'No, very cool.'

'Chel, that's even worse.' He switched on the intercom.

'I have got very little to say to you, Dom, except to remind you of your duty to the planet. Doesn't it mean anything to you? You may be killed.'

Dom took a deep breath. 'I may be killed anyway. At least there's no false sense of security here.'

'Fool! You are just seizing the chance to jaunt off on an idiot quest. And incidentally, there's a shape-war brewing down here. Half a squad of guards have been slaughtered in the *buruku*. The one at Tau City is on fire—'

'Samhedi took his men in with stunners. You know guns are against all phnobic law.'

There was a pause. Dom glanced at the screen. The pall over Tau City had grown. As he watched, a point well to the west of the City suddenly flashed into a streak of blinding light. The sunlight had reached the Jokers Tower.

'That was . . . foolish,' said Joan slowly. 'Nevertheless, officers of the Board are entitled to some respect. I'm declaring a State of Emergency. A ship will pick you up within the hour.'

Dom cut the connection and spun round to Hrsh-Hgn.

'Can you get through to the leader of all the *burukus*? The Servant of the Pillar, isn't it?'

'You know not what you assk. However—'

In three minutes Dom was looking at a screen holding the image of a small, lightly built phnobe, wearing a silver collar. A female? Phnobes were generally reticent about their sex.

'On behalf of the Board,' he said, 'what may we do to repair this grievous hurt?'

The Servant hissed. 'The soil of the *buruku* has been disgraced.' Dom nodded. The *bururu* was covered to a depth of several inches with Phnobic soil, specially transported.

'We could replace it,' he said.

They haggled. Finally Dom concluded the conversation with a suitable expression of regard and said: 'It'll cost us several hundred thousand standards in haulage charges alone.'

'Can you authorize Board expenditure?'

'Board expenditure nothing. It'll come out of the Sabalos personal account.' He sat back, suddenly tired.

'There is another problem,' said Isaac from his seat. 'Like, where are we going? And how are we going to get there?'

'Hrsh?'

The phnobe pinched his nose. 'The First Sirian Bank would make a good starting point. According to legend he was created by the Jokers.'

'Oh. I hadn't heard that. And he's my god-father.'

'Well, it issn't true. He iss at least three billion yearss old, ass far as he knows.'

Isaac whistled. There was something on the

deep radar, drifting purposely towards the ship.

'It's a sundog, touting for business,' said Dom. 'There's our passage to Sirius.'

'Count me out!' shrieked the phnobe. 'I'm not travelling on one of thosse animalss! I thought this sship had an interspace matrix!'

'It had,' said Isaac calmly. 'It probably worked real good in Dom's great-great-grandfather's day but now the settings are all anyhow. Fancy ending up inside a star? Think of the loss to letters.'

'Very well then. But under sstrong protesst.'

Twenty minutes later a shadow eclipsed the stars. The sundog stopped a few hundred metres from the ship, a fat lozenge flashing like a beacon as it turned slowly in the sunlight.

Isaac peered into the scope.

'It has orange, purple and yellow markings, boss, with a black band across the yellow.'

Dom sighed with relief. Not all sundogs were friendly, or bright enough to realize what would follow if they forgot themselves and engulfed a small spaceship.

'That will be the one who calls itself Abramelin-lincoln-stroke-Enobarbous-stroke-50.3-Enobarbous-McMirmidom,' he said. 'He's okay. He does haulage work for us.'

A thought stole unbidden into his head.

Hullo, spaceman. You wish to travel, maybe?

'Please take us to the First Sirian Bank.'

Price for journey: seventeen standards.

The ship bucked slightly as the sundog reached out and enveloped it in a pseudofield. The giant semi-animal rotated slowly to face the actinic blue star, inasmuch as a sundog had a face.

'This is undignified,' moaned Hrsh-Hgn. 'Carried by a dog like so much freight.'

To be ready.

'Would you rather Grandmother caught us, in her present mood?'

To be steady.

'Frssh!'

'Come on, now, face it like a cosmopolitan.'

Go.

An invisible hand wrenched See-Why out of the sky and hurled it at them. They were falling into the sun. Then they were falling around the sun. They skimmed over a blurred sea of blue-white fire that broke on the reefs of space, its roaring a dim thunder inside the pseudofield, towards a glowing horizon that had no curve.

And the star dopplered behind them. Sundog soared up into the interstellar dark, singing.

Silence filled the cabin.

'Wow,' said Dom.

'Urghss!'

Isaac peered at the matrix panel, and dimmed the ship lights. In the darkness there were only the stars ahead, and they began to flare blue.

'Prepare yourselves to become a relativistic impossibility . . .' sang Isaac.

Illusion.

Dom knew about the things seen in interspace. The larger ships usually had screening around most of the hull, and perhaps an unscreened lounge for the incurably curious . . .

A white stag galloped through the cabin wall, which glowed under an orange light. It bore a gold crown between its horns. Dom sensed its fear, smelled the rankness, saw the sweat-matted hair on its flanks – but its hooves merged with the floor, and floor and skin merged and flowed continuously. It reared, and leapt through the autochef.

Dom saw the huntsman on his black horse when he brushed through the wall of the drive cabin like bracken. He wore white, except for a red cloak hung with silver bells, and his face beneath yellow hair that billowed in an intangible wind was pale and set. For a moment he looked at Dom, who saw his eyes gleam momentarily like mirrors and a hand go up protectively. Then horse and rider were gone.

'Chel! He almost seemed real!'

Isaac grinned. 'He almost certainly is, somewhere.'

'Uhuh. They say interspace is where all possibilities intersect. I got the feeling he sensed us.'

'A spirit on the wind, no more.'

Dom stood up unsteadily. The walls still looked as if they had been made of second-hand moonlight.

'Now there's an illusion I've heard about.'

A red globe the size of a fist drifted easily through the shielded windows. He watched fascinated as it passed through the autochef, part of the main cable conduit, and the floating figure of Ig, who stirred uneasily in his sleep. It disappeared in the general direction of the matrix computer.

It was an interspace interpretation of a star, probably BD+6793°. They were harmless enough, though a red giant or a spitting white dwarf could be unnerving to watch as it passed through your body.

Dom looked round after hearing a scuffle. Hrsh-Hgn was wedged under the autochef, in the foetal position. It was almost an hour before he was persuaded to emerge, blinking with embarrassment.

'We phnobess are not perhapss so ressilient ass you—' he began. 'Intersspace sscares uss. It is a region of uncertainty. Who knowss that we may not ceasse to exist?'

'You appear to be all here, physically and mentally.'

The phnobe nodded sheepishly.

Isaac closed the maintenance panel on the autochef.

'It's a '706 model, a quality job,' he said. 'I can't find a printout for the menu, anywhere.'

Dom nodded. 'I think Great-great-grandfather intended the *One Jump* as a one-man ship. I should imagine the menu is programmed into it.'

'Quite. He'd be so busy fleeing from his creditors he'd have no time— Sorry, chief, I think maybe I stepped out of line a little there.'

'It's okay. He was a bit of a pirate. But according to the family history he was a strict Sadhimist, too. Simplicity was a virtue. I shouldn't expect it to run to anything more appetizing than bread and maybe fish.'

The autochef used simple molecule-breeding techniques to duplicate dishes stored as probability equations in its menu. The one aboard *One Jump Ahead* gurgled after it was switched on, broke into a low buzz for several minutes, and extruded a table from a base slot. Another, larger slot opened and the meal slid out.

They stared at it for several seconds. Dom reached out and picked up a crystallized fruit, gingerly.

Hrsh-Hgn coughed. 'The intricate bird with the honey glaze I recognize,' he murmured. 'It's a Croupier swan. I think the blobss are cream.'

Dom took the lid off a silver dish.

'Some class of a shellfish baked in— Well, it tastes of eggs.'

Isaac picked up a cut-glass goblet and downed the contents in one swallow.

'Old Overcoat,' he said. 'The genuine stuff. Two glasses and you lift off on a pillar of flame.'

They stared at him. He put down the glass.

'Haven't you seen a robot drink before?' he asked.

'We were wondering . . .' Dom stopped, embarrassed.

'. . . where it goesss?'

'We new model Class Fives can derive power from the calorific content of organic substances.' He reached for his chest panel. 'If you like I can—'

'We believe you,' said Dom. He looked down at the table again. 'Did I say something about the virtues of simplicity? I think it may be against Sadhimist laws to eat this.'

' "You will not waste",' quoted Hrsh-Hgn. 'There are timess when it iss a pleassure as well ass a duty to follow the One Commandment.'

Ten minutes later, Dom said: 'Hrsh-Hgn, this damn black jam tastes of fish.'

'It's caviar.'

'Caviar? I'd always wondered. On Widdershins only poor people are allowed to eat it. I suppose they get used to it.'

Twenty minutes later the autochef digested the remains of the meal. Ig drifted towards the matrix room, chewing a fish head. A small, burned-out wreck of a star passed crosswise through the cabin and disappeared. Dom watched it go.

'If the First Sirian Bank is the galaxy's leading Joker expert, why hasn't he found Jokers World?' he asked.

'I assume you don't mean that he should have

97

roved across the universe, Roche limits being what they are. A thing the ssize of the Bank would upset the balance of the average solar system, probably. As to exploration via the available data, he may well have disscovered Jokerss World. Why not? Why, then, sshould he tell uss, mere upstart civilissationss?'

'We'd pay well.'

'We? *We*? Phnobic *We*? Human *We*? Let uss assume the race who findss Jokerss World gains immeasurably. Why should he want that?'

Dom frowned. 'But he runs himself as a Bank. He charges for his services, too.'

'He choosess to. A creature musst do something to relieve the boredom of three billion years. He likes people around.'

'You mean he wouldn't like to see anyone get hold of the World because they might put the Bank in jeopardy?'

'Maybe. It iss all conjecture.'

He started to talk about Jokers World.

Three races walked like men. One of them was Man. Taller than men, but generally lighter, were the phnobes. Much smaller than men, but built more on cuboid lines so that they looked like heavy-gravity chimpanzees on a steroid diet, were drosks.

Phnobes came in three sexes. They had a secondary, vestigial brain. They evolved on a world with no readily available metal. In cerebral matters they were supreme. A world where most of the higher animals were adapted to a tri-sexual system needed a race with brains.

Drosks came in two sexes, eventually. It made sense on a harsh, bitter world. The young males evolved into mature, strong-minded females after about the first third of their life. Their social system was intricate but was surpassed in complexity by their religion, a fiery edifice involving the double star and three large moons in their system. Drosks were cannibals, it was part of the religion. Drosks found it difficult to conceive of a number greater than seven. Drosks periodically built up a machine-age civilization then, for no well-understood reason, carefully dismantled it and reverted to barbarism.

Compared to all the other fifty-two races known, drosks, phnobes and men were like brothers. To some races, like the Spooners who lived on little icy worlds, they were merely identical. Many others would be incapable of thinking of them as life at all – like say, the Tarquins, who lived in the upper layers of some protostars.

A few races had a large conception of life. The Creapii lived on small, hot worlds, in the deep layers of the larger gas giants and occasionally on the surface of very cool suns, but could discourse on philosophy with men as easily as they could discuss the untranslatable with

99

Tarquins. Then there were the sundogs, who were merely raw life and derived their picture of the universe from the minds of their customers. The First Sirian Bank was in a class of his own, as always. A few races – The Pod, for one – were alien even to Spooners and Tarquins.

But all the races had one thing in common. They were all less than five million years old, and all had originated within a sphere of stars less than 200 light years across, centred on Wolf 429. The Creapii discovered that first, and so were the first to investigate the one planet that orbited the Wolf.

They found a Joker tower, a monomolecular spire frosted with frozen methane, standing dark and alone under the airless sky. They found the thing later known simply as the Centre of the Universe.

The Creapii ranged far. They found more towers, other Joker artefacts like the Ring Stars, Band and the Internal Planets of Protostar V. As an incidental, they found Earth and sold a working matrix motor for homesteading rights on Mercury. The Creapii were beginning to feel in the grip of a galactic mystery, and had long before decided that they needed extra insights.

Seventy standard years later a joint Man-Phnobe team deciphered Joker Curiform C, the only one of the five Joker scripts translatable. There were hints of a great civilization, although

100

the word was only an approximation, and there was probably the first poem in the universe.

Geological evidence suggested that the towers were all between eight and five million years old. They were ranged more or less equally across the light years, accepting all energies, radiating none.

The Creapii knew that they had recognizably evolved from the mildly intelligent salamanders about four million years before, to judge from the desiccated aluminium-polysilicate remains on their planet around 70 Ophiuchis A. They knew of no race older.

They were long-lived. They had travelled up the Tentacle – Creapii mythology saw the galaxy as a giant Creap, with a glittering carcase of stars – to the sparse stars at the rim. They had sailed down the Tentacle to the cathedral of stars at the hub. The stars were barren. There were one or two freak accidents. But generally, life was still merely some slightly more complex chemical changes. Only in the bubble of stars behind them did worlds teem.

Impetuous races would have reached a definite conclusion hastily, maybe in two or three hundred years. The Creap minds, of which each individual had three, did not jump so readily to conclusions . . .

'And what conclusion did they reach?' asked Dom.

'The Creapii are powerful, and slow, and

thorough. They have as yet reached no conclusion. They are seeking the meaning of life.
Why sshould they hurry?'

'Chel! Isn't the theory that the Jokers seeded
our stars before they – uh – moved away? Come
on, you know it is.'

The phnobe nodded slowly. 'That is certainly
the hypothesis that the Joker Institute appears to
work on.'

Dom bit his lip, and opened his mouth to
speak. Hrsh-Hgn raised a hand.

'You are about to assk why. Boy, remember
that of fifty-two races in the life-stars you, an
Earthman—'

'A Widdershine!'

'True, a Widdershine of Earth stock – can
only vaguely understand the mental workings of
perhaps three or four races. Why should we
hope to understand the Jokers?'

'But the Institute did understand Joker
Curiform C. It was one of their languages.'

'Yes, but a written language is merely a
machine to convey information, and once we
had the key it was remarkably easy to translate.'

'How was it broken?'

'They used a poet, and a mad computer.'

Hrsh-Hgn picked up the cube of pink silica
that had been his present to Dom, thumbed
the reference face and set it to project. The
words of the Joker Testament hung in the air,
glowing.

You who stand before us
We have held the stars in the hollow
Of our hands, and the stars
Burn. Pray be careful now
As to how you handle them.
We have gone to wait on our new world
There is but one
It lies at the dark side of the sun.

'Pretty derivative stuff,' said Isaac. 'That last couplet is really a singlet.'

'I must admit it is better in phnobic,' said Hrsh-Hgn. 'As for the rest, well, you musst know most of it. On a purely practical level, hotheads have searched every sizeable body in the bubble and many out of it.'

'Now we're getting down to the nitty-gritty,' said Isaac. 'You'd have had to include suns, of course, and the deeps themselves. Although it sounds more likely that the Jokers originated on-planet somewhere.'

'The popular belief is that Jokers World is laden with wonders beyond belief,' said Hrsh-Hgn.

'Sitting in here it's hard to get some idea of the deeps, but they must be big enough to hide a world in. The Jokers might have had a world with no sun,' said Dom.

'It's just conceivable,' agreed Hrsh-Hgn, politely.

'It's been thought of, huh?'

'About once every five years.'

'How about it being invisible?' said Isaac. Dom laughed.

'Maybe,' said Hrsh-Hgn. 'You'd heard of ghost stars, Dom?'

'Uhuh. So dense that not even gravity escapes from them.'

'Now this is just an idea to kick about, I'm just dropping it on the plate to see if anyone pours mayonnaise on it, but you could outfit an entire solar system with matrix engines and drop it into interspace,' said Isaac. Dom was about to laugh, but looked sidelong at Hrsh-Hgn.

'That's the legend of the Prodigal Sun,' said Hrsh-Hgn. 'A low-temperature Creapii story. Yes, you could do it in about fifty years' time, at our present rate of technological expanssion. The catalytic power would not have to be too great. But the practical application of the matrix equation makes it impossible.' He caught Dom's blank expression. 'You see, you do not need a great deal of power to drop even a large mass in and out of interspace.'

Hrsh-Hgn used more technical language to explain that it was the on-board computer that really counted. Since a body in interspace was theoretically everywhere at the same time and would if randomly dropped out almost certainly materialize in the centre of the nearest solar body, the navigational matrix computer was very necessary. It had to be big – 'everywhere' was a large volume to be quantified. The bigger the body, the greater chance of error, so the bigger the computer.

'The sundog carrying us now registered a current drain in microamps to achieve interspace. It's little more than a mental discipline. Four-fifths of its body iss a hindbrain designed to locate it accurately with regard to the datum universse, with fortunately just enough sspare capacity to allow for the extra mass of a medium-ssized sship.

'To get a medium-range star successfully through interspace you'd have to have a computer about one hundred times its mass.'

'How about one planet?' asked Dom.

'The graphs meet at planets like Phnobis or Widdershins, small and dense. You could just about do it if you hollowed out the world and filled it with computers. But this is a fruitless line of ssspeculation. Personally I believe that the Jokers—'

Illusion.

Ig was keening. Dom opened his eyes and blinked. He was soaked in sweat. One arm ached.

At the far end of the cabin Hrsh-Hgn had been thrown like a doll across the gear locker.

'Isaac?'

The robot let go of the handrail that ringed *One Jump*'s cabin.

'Rough, huh?' he asked.

'I feel like someone just hit me with something large, like a planet,' said Dom. 'Or a large asteroid. What's happened?'

'We're between stars. It looks as though the sundog dropped out rather clumsily.'

Dom floated up, trying to quieten his stomach. It appeared to be knotted. His head ached.

Hrsh-Hgn groaned and woke. 'Frghsss—' he swore.

'Sundog?' said Dom to the empty air.

Apologies. Journey interrupted owing to circumstances beyond control. Disturbance in interspace matrix spaceframe. We must detour in datum space.

Isaac was glued to the deep radar.

'It's still several million kilometres away – it must be throwing one hell of an interspace shadow. It's taking its time. It's a cone – oh, my, will you look at that!'

They stared into the screen. On maximum magnification it showed a pyramid tumbling deceptively slowly through space, flashing faintly as starlight caught its polished faces. There was no mistaking the outline of a Joker tower.

Dom swam into the pilot seat and asked the sundog to take them in closer. In a few minutes they were a few kilometres away. The tower hung steady against a starfield that spun like a mad planetarium.

'The Institute of Joker Studies pays a million standards bounty for details of new towers,' said Dom. 'I want to catch it.'

'In a pig's eye,' said Isaac. 'That mass at that speed? It's a job for twenty sundogs.'

Right.

'Well, we can plot its course. There's a reduced bounty for that sort of information. We could split it three ways.'

Four ways.

'Okay, four—'

Dom struggled for breath. Something had caught him in a vice, and was squeezing hard.

He sensed the ship. He was acutely aware of the convoluted atomic structure of the hull. The little deuterium pile in the matrix computer sparkled like a witch ball left over from Hogswatchnight. Isaac was a coruscation of currents flowing over coiled alloy wire, suffused with the sickening feel of metallic hydrogen. The sundog brain throbbed dull purple with vague semi-thoughts.

Beyond the ship, beyond the tumbling tower, he felt the other ship. It was waiting for him. Someone had known that he would pass under this area. He felt metallic hydrogen again – the feel of a robot mind.

He felt inside the sundog's mind. There was a jolt as its field polarized and the tower receded instantly against the stars. For a moment he felt the rage of the mind in the other ship. Then it was gone, lost in the static as the sundog sank gratefully into interspace.

And something withdrew from his mind, gently. He had time for a very brief feeling of loss, of the unfair restriction of a mere five senses . . . then the reaction hit him.

He didn't fall, because there was no 'down'. But he hung bewildered, listening to the puzzled protests from the sundog. Hrsh-Hgn and Isaac were staring at him. Then the phnobe took him gently in one bony hand and hauled him down to the bunk.

'I saw everything,' muttered Dom. 'Something was *looking* through me, there was an assassin waiting at that tower, you know . . .'

'Ssure,' murmured Hrsh-Hgn. 'Ssure.'

'Believe me!'

'Ssure.'

'He had a molecule stripper!' shouted Dom.

'Something made the sundog get the hell out of there,' admitted Isaac. 'Was it you?'

Dom nodded violently, and then added slowly: 'I think so. But – but just before, I saw . . . Would you believe I saw probabilities? I saw us powdered by that stripper. But that was in another universe. We escaped, in this one. Chel, I can't describe it. We haven't got the right words!'

6

'We have given this case a great deal of thought. We do, of course, find nothing to argue with in the purely geophysical reports put before us. We note that this world known as the First Sirian Bank is a planet with a diameter of seven thousand miles and a crust consisting almost entirely of crystalline silicon and some associated elements. We have also heard some delightful evidence from Dr Al Putachique of Earth, its import being that over the billennia earthquakes and so forth have caused the formation of billions of transistor junctions within that crust, forming by natural means the largest computer in the galaxy. We are of course aware that the Bank has for many years been used as the accounting-house and general information repository of most of the Human and near-Human races, and is officially Treasurer of the Star Chamber of Commerce.

'The appellant has asked for the legal status of Human. He wishes to be accorded the status of living creature. Is the Bank alive? By every definition he is not. That, at least, is what we have been told.

'But we disagree. It has been impossible for the Bank to be physically present here today, Roche limits being what they are, but this Chamber has spoken with him at length. Towards the end of this unusual interlude my colleague from Earth made a reference, I understand it to be from some kind of theatrical entertainment, to the fact that it seemed unfair that the merest virus should have life while the Bank had none at all.

'We find it nowhere stated that an entire world may not be accorded the status of a living creature, or even of Human. It may be a trifle unusual, a little irregular. Nevertheless, let it be recorded that we find the First Sirian Bank not only alive, but possessed of a universe-view sufficiently advanced to call him Human. And may his orbit never grow less.'

His Furness CrAAgh 456°, Mediator, the Star Chamber, 2104. (See also *Life: A Legal Definition* by His Furness 456°.)

Dom dodged into a booth and waited a minute before glancing out through the clear crystal panel of the door. There were two or three thousand people in the central hall, but none seemed to have noticed him.

In front of him was a black crystal wall, studded with innumerable pinpoints of red light. They clustered thickly around a plain copper disc, set flush with the crystal. It hummed, said: 'Please state your business.'

Dom relaxed.

'Are you the Bank?' he asked.

'No, sir. I am a Teller, merely a comparatively simple servo-mechanical subunit.'

'Uh, okay. Then please transfer seventeen standards to the sundog racial account,' he said, while invisible eyes tactfully examined his retinal patterns, voice inflections, DNA helix and teeth.

'Transaction completed.'

'And I wish to notify the Joker Institute that I have located a Joker building, description and position as noted.'

He pressed a copy of the *One Jump*'s log into a recess below the disc.

'Bounty will be paid on verification.'

Dom wondered if the assassin lurking at the tower had also registered discovery. He *knew* there had been an assassin. Somewhere in totality was a universe where Dom Sabalos was dead. But of course, there would be many such universes. According to p-math there was at least one universe for every probability, even the unthinkable ones.

'Business completed?' asked the disc.

Dom frowned. It was his first visit to the Bank,

although it was officially his godfather. The Bank sent him greetings on the appropriate ceremonies, like his minor twenty-eighth-year birthdays, and small, interesting presents like the gravity sandals he was still wearing. The gifts suggested a thoughtful personality. The greetings cards told nothing at all, except that they were generally signed in crescive High-Degree Creapii IV, a favourite script for multi-dextral amateur calligraphers. The problem now was making contact.

'I am Dom Sabalos, the Bank's godson. I would like to see him.'

'You have only to look around, sir.' The machine meant it seriously. Dom realized it was not equipped to handle figurative speech.

'I meant that I wanted to confront him, converse with his, uh, seat of consciousness.'

There was a pause. At last the disc said: 'Very well, sir, I will see what can be arranged.'

Dom hurried out of the booth. Hrsh-Hgn was lurking suspiciously behind a glittering germanian pillar that soared up half a mile above the paved cavern floor. The next essential was fresh clothing, and then a real meal – there was something curiously unsatisfying about the reconstituted molecules of the ship's auto-chef. He pushed past a party of medium-degree Creapii and hailed a cab.

The main cavern of the First Sirian Bank was big enough to need a sophisticated weather control system, to prevent the formation of thunderclouds. The cab looped up from the crowded floor and threaded its way at speed between coruscating pillars, each with its cluster of booths at the base. The red junction points glowed everywhere. Occasionally a ring of static electricity would flash up a pillar and burst vividly into an ozone-reeking haze. And the hot dry air hummed with a million voices, felt rather than heard, as money spoke to money across the light years.

In fact, Dom considered, it looked like an early conception of Hell. With tourists. Certainly some of the tourists would have fitted the concept nicely.

In one of the sub-caverns a robot tailor outfitted him with an anonymous grey ship suit, the sort worn on every earth-human world. He also bought a cuber, a cloak striped on the bias in purple, orange and yellow, and hoped that an observer would take him for what he appeared to be – a back-planet rube, a stock Whole Erse character of comedy sketches, the gawping rim-colonist with a nasal twang, unfortunate personal habits and a pocketful of rare earths.

He turned and looked critically at Hrsh-Hgn, who stood watching in the old ceremonial garb of a beta-male.

'Couldn't you wear something a bit more colourful? Some phnobes do. I'd rather you didn't look conspicuous.'

Hrsh-Hgn took a nervous step backwards and clutched at his robe.

'Is it against the law? I mean, will it offend some sexual *more*? If so, of course, I—'

'It'ss not exactly that. I do not think I could carry off the character of an alpha, you understand, they are somewhat more flamboyant, more warlike, lesss given to featss of the intellect . . .'

At Dom's command the little robot dressed the phnobe in a complicated toga of heavy blue and olive-green fibres, shot with flecks of silver. A tshuri knife fully twice the length of Hrsh-Hgn's old one hung on an ornate belt.

'If an alpha challenges me I shall make a poor showing.'

'Still, you look different.' He paid the robot, and they walked out with Hrsh-Hgn making a brave attempt at a swagger.

The temperate lifeforms dining room of the Grand Hotel, the only provision on the Bank for accommodation, seemed almost as big as the main cavern and more impressive because the size was made up in human terms. The long cavern was filled with the roar of appetites in the process of satiation, reeked with the aromas of many foods and narcotics, and looked rather more like Hell than the main cavern.

Dom found two places at a table in the Human section. The previous occupants, a thickset Earthman with a face criss-crossed with duelling scars and a small battered Class One robot, nodded familiarly at Dom as they passed.

'Do you know them?' asked Hrsh-Hgn as they sat down.

'Not that I can recall,' said Dom. 'There's something odd about them. He looked a wealthy type. What's he doing with a mere Class One?'

'One of life'ss little myssteriess,' said the phnobe.

They ate in silence. The diner beside Dom was energetically digging him in the ribs with a horny elbow. It was a young drosk, who looked up, gave Dom a canine grin, and bent back to his plate. Dom carefully refrained from looking at what he was eating.

On the other side a party of female phnobes of the Long Cloud group were arguing sibilantly. Beyond them was a Pineal-human, performing a complex Third Eye food ceremony over his rice bowl.

Dom ordered fish and bread. Hrsh-Hgn had a fungi stew.

The Class Two waiter trundled up with their bill and tactfully ascertained Dom's credit rating with the Bank.

'Divert a tenth-standard for yourself,' added Dom.

'Many thanks indeed, sir,' said the automaton. It added politely: 'I have always had a high regard for Sinistral-humans, sir.'

'Who said I was from Widdershins?' Dom

115

tried to pitch his voice low. Several of the phnobes looked round. But the robot had rolled away.

'Your face,' said Hrsh-Hgn simply.

Dom reached up, and then caught sight of his hand. The greenish tinge of googoo. Of course it was used on other worlds in exceptional circumstances – and under strict licence – but that made no difference. In popular mythology, any green man was a Widdershine.

'I don't think you need bother too much,' said the phnobe as they walked out. 'Whoever thiss asssasssin iss, I doubt if he will be fooled by dissguises. He iss using probability math to put himself in the right place every time.'

'He's not succeeded so far. Remember what happened at that tower?'

'Don't bank on it.'

A small two-wheel Class One trundled towards them and tugged at Dom's cloak.

'Lord Sabalos, Bank will see you now. To follow me.'

It rolled away on its balloon tyres. They followed it at a walking pace.

Dom looked around him and made no attempt to disguise his awe. He was beginning to feel like a rube anyway. The times he had left See-Why's system were few enough, but he closed his mouth firmly when he found it was hanging open.

The main cavern had been opened out near

the North Temperate Fault, the result of an ancient computer quake that had slid two continent-sized silicon slabs together and created several quintillion important circuits. It had happened when Earth was still molten. Historians suggested that it had marked the awakening of the Bank; the colossal, thundering moment between dead piezoelectric rock and sapience. On this point, as on many concerning its personal history, the Bank was silent.

The robot led them up a shallow slope against the Fault and into a branching tunnel hewn from the living – it was a fair statement – rock. The pinpoints clustered thickly here.

A sphincter door opened. They went in.

'DOM! COME RIGHT IN!'

The room was small and brightly lit. Thick carpets covered the floor and there was a large potted palm in the corner. Against the far wall was a desk, simply furnished. A robot sat behind it. It had been stripped of most of its outer casing, including its head, and was strung about with auxiliary equipment. Ropes of cables connected it to the wall. It was smoking a cigar through an extended tube.

'GREETINGS TO YOU, TOO, HRSH-HGN.'

Dom stared at the cigar.

'NOT PRIMARILY AN AFFECTATION,' said the Bank. 'THERE IS A CERTAIN SENSUAL PLEASURE, YOU UNDERSTAND. AND IT HELPS TO PUT SOME OF MY MORE NERVOUS VISITORS AT THEIR EASE. A

ROBOT IS HUMANOID. WHEN ON TOP OF THAT IT IS SMOKING A CIGAR IT IS FAR MORE RELAXING TO CONVERSE WITH THAN—'

'—a planet-sized computer?' suggested Dom. 'Hello, Godfather.'

'I TRUST YOUR FAMILY IS IN GOOD HEALTH.'

'Reasonably so, when I left Widdershins,' said Dom. 'It's very good of you to see us.'

'NOT AT ALL. I ALWAYS HAVE TIME FOR MY GODCHILDREN. AND HRSH-HGN, OF COURSE, ONE OF THE MORE PROMISING AMATEUR STUDENTS OF THE JOKER MYSTERY.'

Hrsh-Hgn nodded graciously.

'Godchildren?' asked Dom, interested despite himself. 'I . . . uh . . . thought I was the only one.'

'I HAVE SEVERAL THOUSAND. IT PLEASES ME TO SEE THEM GROW UP AND MAKE THEIR WAY IN THE UNIVERSE. AND NOW, DOM, THE SUBJECT CONCERNING WHICH YOU NO DOUBT CAME HERE TO CONSULT ME.'

The red lights in the wall flared.

'I REFER TO THE ATTEMPTS ON YOUR LIFE, YOUR FATHER'S PREDICTIONS, AND YOUR CURRENT QUEST. THE FAILED ASSASSINATIONS, FIRST.'

Dom told his story. Occasionally the light patterns would change. At last the robot laid down the cigar and the Bank spoke.

'THERE IS, YOU REALIZE, ONE COMFORTING ASPECT. THESE ATTEMPTS FAILED. THAT SUGGESTS A FALLIBLE AGENT.'

Dom sat back. 'Yes, but the failures weren't – I

118

mean, they were not natural. Something happened. I feel like a tstame puppet, as if I was being moved about by a couple of players just so that I could fulfil some prediction.'

'BUT YOU READILY SET OUT TO FIND JOKERS WORLD, WITHOUT FORETHOUGHT.'

He tried to think of an intelligent answer. None was forthcoming. Why had he been so ready? He was scared, yes, and wanted to run away. There was most of the galaxy to see. It was an adventure. But he had to admit there was more to it.

'It seemed the right thing at the time. I can't explain why,' he said, simply.

'YOU ACCEPTED FATE. A PHNOBE WOULD SAY "BATER". A PHILOSOPHIC DROSK WOULD SAY YOU HEARD TODAY'S ECHO OF TOMORROW'S SCREAM. YOU ACTED OUT OF UNCONSCIOUS FOREKNOWLEDGE.'

Dom's shirt moved and Ig poked his head out and blinked at the lights.

'AS FAR AS WIDDERSHINS IS CONCERNED, I FIND NO REASON WHY YOU SHOULD BE KILLED. AS FAR AS SENIOR PLANETARY MANAGEMENT IS CONCERNED, THERE ARE FAR WORSE IN THE GALAXY.

'I HAVE BEEN RUNNING A PROBABILITY PROGRAM ON YOU FOR SEVERAL SECONDS. IT APPEARS THAT YOU WILL DISCOVER JOKERS WORLD. NOW THERE IS A GENERAL BELIEF THAT THE JOKER INSTITUTE SEEKS OUT AND KILLS ALL

THOSE IT PREDICTS MAY DISCOVER JOKERS WORLD. BUT THAT IS MERE CONJECTURE.'

Behind Dom Hrsh-Hgn hissed softly.

'YOU DON'T SEEM SURPRISED.'

He felt the phnobe's soup-plate eyes on him as he said carefully: 'I know I will discover Jokers World. I knew when I heard my father say so. I . . . felt things lock into place. I will discover Jokers World. That's why I set out. It's the most important thing that I must do. No one can stop me.'

He was surprised to hear his voice. But he felt the certainty nestling securely in his mind now.

And the certainty faded, like a dream. It left him mouthing, blushing. He felt Hrsh-Hgn's hand on his shoulder. Ig looked up at him, with his head on one side.

For a few seconds the robot voice-box merely emitted a faint static hiss. Then the Bank spoke kindly in a softer voice.

'DON'T BET YOUR LIFE ON CERTAINTIES, DOM. BEWARE OF HUBRIS.'

Hrsh-Hgn leaned forward. In a voice slightly louder than necessary he said: 'Reason suggests that if Jokers World exisstss in the life-bubble it would have been found. I know one myth which ssayss they live on the core of Procyon, where even Creapii may not go. What do you say to thiss?'

'AS A MATTER OF FACT, I WAS INTERESTED IN

YOUR THEORY AS PUT FORWARD IN YOUR RECENT CUBE.'

'Your theory, Hrsh?' said Dom. 'You didn't tell me!'

'We were interrupted by that tower, remember?'

'IT WAS A NEAT EXTRAPOLATION ON THE PHRASE "THE DARK SIDE OF THE SUN". IT WOULD INVOLVE FINDING A BINARY STAR, OF THE EPSILON AURIGAE TYPE,' the Bank explained.

Three minutes later Dom said: 'I understand the idea. And the Creapii use sun rafts on some stars.'

'IT IS CERTAINLY THE ONLY CASE WHERE A SUN HAS A DARK SIDE. THERE ARE, HOWEVER, MANY BINARIES OF THAT TYPE, AND A SYSTEMIC SEARCH WOULD BE TIME-CONSUMING.'

'I gather you don't agree with my ssuggesstion?' said Hrsh-Hgn thoughtfully.

'I PRAISE IT AS IMAGINATIVE THINKING OF THE HIGHEST ORDER,' intoned the Bank carefully.

'Iss it true that the Jokerss helped you evolve, as the legend sayss?'

'I DO NOT ANSWER PERSONAL QUESTIONS. THERE IS ONE FACTOR YOU MIGHT CONSIDER. WHY NOT RUN AN EXTENDED SET OF EQUATIONS ON DOM AND DISCOVER EXACTLY WHEN AND WHERE HE MAKES HIS DISCOVERY? I HAVE JUST RUN AN ANALYSIS TAKING AS ITS PARAMETER THE EXISTENCE OF JOKERS WORLD AND ITS IMMINENT DISCOVERY. I FIND I ARRIVE AT THE MANTRUM:

ncreg8
(bRf) (nultad) E YY –'   (=) 56:::   nultad
tt:
al

'THIS IS ONLY A FIRST-APPROXIMATION DISTIL-
LATE.'

Hrsh-Hgn pulled a notecube out of his small
carry-all, and gazed at it carefully.

'What value do you give the datum?' he asked.

'Ae(d) IN THE USUAL SUB-LUNAR MATRIX.'

'Then that ressultss in an almosst perfect
collapsed field within the next twenty-seven
days.'

'EXCELLENT. I DID NOT KNOW HIGHER PROB-
ABILITY WAS A PHNOBIC SPECIALITY.'

'It iss, you understand, in accordance with our
universse-view.'

Dom had wandered over to the potted palm
and was fingering a leaf idly. It moved under
his touch, betraying itself as a vegetative shape-
changer from Eggplant. He let go quickly, and
stroked Ig.

'I don't begin to understand,' he said, flatly.
'To me it sounds like Jargon.'

'JARGON?'

Hrsh-Hgn turned to the Bank. 'Nonsense,' he
explained. 'In Sadhimist tradition God invented
it to foresstall the firsst attempt at intersstellar
travel. To prevent scientissts from understanding
each other, you understand. You will find it

mentioned in the Newer Testament.'

The pinpoints swam into a new position. The robot extension gave a mechanical gurgle.

'AH YES. AS WE SPREAD OUR CIRCUITRY LESS ESSENTIAL INFORMATION . . . YOU UNDERSTAND HOW IT IS.'

The Jokers did not show up on p-math. It was as if they never existed. P-math offered no explanation for the towers or the other artefacts. Wherever the Jokers had been they left a shadow in the equations.

Dom's future was sure for twenty-seven standard days.

'That's something to look forward to,' said Dom. 'How about giving me a little hint about its whereabouts?'

'EVERY INHABITED BODY IN THE HOME BUBBLE HAS BEEN THOROUGHLY EXPLORED. I SUGGEST A FRUITFUL FIELD OF EXPLORATION IS YOUR OWN MIND. HOWEVER, YOU MAY CARE TO SEEK OUT HIM WHO LIVES ON BAND. HE IS OLD. HE HAS MET THE JOKERS.'

'But Band is unoccupied except by sundogs – it's been proved it could never develop a higher lifeform.'

'I HAVE SAID TOO MUCH.'

'Well, will you work on the problem of my assassin?'

The Bank paused. 'YES.'

'Charge it to my personal account.'

'I WILL DO SO. IT IS A PITY YOU WERE NOT HERE

EARLIER. THE GREATEST AUTHORITY ON THE JOKERS, AND CERTAINLY THE MOST INCISIVE MIND IN THE GALAXY, WAS HERE.'

The atmosphere was perceptibly warmer. Dom relaxed. The Bank was hiding something, though.

'I thought you were the most incisive mind in the galaxy,' he said.

'A COMMON MISTAKE. ALAS, I AM NO MORE INTELLIGENT THAN THE AVERAGE CREAP, OR HUMAN GENIUS. MY BULK ALLOWS, SHALL WE SAY, FOR BREADTH OF INTELLIGENCE RATHER THAN HEIGHT. I WAS REFERRING TO CHARLES SUB-LUNAR.'

' "Poet, polymath, soldier of fortune",' quoted Dom. 'Was he the man I saw in the hotel? Scarred, he was, with an early Class One robot?'

'HE DOES NOT ALLOW HIS LIKENESS TO BE PUBLISHED,' said the Bank, and there was a hint of laughter in the voice.

'Uhuh. I'm getting the hang of things. I don't think seeing him was an accident. I thought he recognized me. He looked rather self-satisfied, so . . .'

'DOM, BECAUSE YOU ARE MY GODSON I WILL RETAIL TO YOU A CERTAIN FACT. YOUR GRAND-MOTHER IS AT THIS MOMENT IN ORBIT ABOVE US, REQUESTING CLEARANCE TO LAND.'

A screen by the robot's arm flashed into life and Dom saw the familiar shape of his grandmother's personal MFTL barge *Drunk*

With Infinity drifting against the stars.

'SHE HAS JUST REFERRED TO ME AS, I QUOTE, A "DISEASED BALL OF ROCK".'

'I'm not certain I want to meet her,' said Dom.

'Mysself neither, my word!'

'THIS COULD BE EXCITING.' A panel in the rock wall ground back. 'THIS IS AN INSPECTION SHAFT. LEAVE THIS WAY. WHERE WILL YOU GO WHEN YOU LEAVE ME?'

'To Band, then, to see this person who is old.'

'AS OLD AS THE HILLS, AS OLD . . .' The Bank paused. There was no sound, but Dom got the distinct impression it was laughing. '. . . AS THE SEA. MOVE!'

Take the Creapii.

Take them as the Jokers. It was an old theory.

They were an ancient race, and they were adaptable. Literally so.

Once there had only been one kind of Creap, the silicon-oxygen Creaps of low degree, living in barbarism and molten phosphorous sulphides on a small world hugging close to the fires of one of the 70 Ophiuchis. Seventeen light years away, a brighter than average ape was seeing real possibilities in banging two stones together.

The Creapii were kindly, patient, and intensely curious. They were also pathologically humble. When they spread into space, they changed the Creap to fit the situation.

Half a million years of gene manipulation and radical molecular restructuring produced the middle-degree Creaps, based on a silicon-carbon bond, a dynamic species that lived happily enough at 500°. Soon afterwards the vats stabilized the intricate aluminium-silicon polymers of the High-Degrees, the ones that occasionally floated their rafts on cool stars.

There were others, including even a boron subspecies. Wherever a star warmed a rock beyond the melting point of tin, there was a Creap to bask in its beneficence.

The Creapii had a long history. They sought knowledge as other, cooler animals sought game. They were polite, and gentlemanly in their dealings. They mixed well. They lived in heat, but had no sexes.

Dom had liked Hrsh-Hgn's theory.

There are many binaries in the galaxy. And often they are an ill-matched pair, one small, dense and actinic, the other huge and red. There is day on the red stars, just occasionally. And there is night on the hemisphere where the bright star does not shine. Dark? There can only be darkness on a sun by contrast.

On this sun the Jokers lived. They . . . would have to be like Creapii, with an armoured integument. Certainly the huge rafts, poised on a heat-contour, would have to be protected. Before the Creapii discovered matrix-power their rafts floated on a down draught of oxidized iron, but the Jokers must have been more inventive . . . a race that twisted the Chain Stars would have to be inventive.

Power would be no problem. Power enough would be very close indeed . . . but it was only a theory . . .

Take men. The Jokers had ceased to build their strange artefacts long before man arose, brother to the apes, but who knew where men had come from? And men were adaptable, or could adapt themselves. There had been a thousand years of colonization. Now the sinistrals of Widdershins had night-black skin, no body hair, a resistance to skin cancers and UV-tolerant eyes. By mere chance, too, half of them were left-handed. On Terra Novae men were stocky and had two hearts. Pineals had more in common with phnobes than other men. The men of Whole Erse lived in a permanent war. Eggplanters were simply strange, and edgy, and vegetarians green in tooth and thorn. And men, it was admitted, were the sort to glory in planet-sized memorials. Weren't the leading Joker experts men?

Spooners could have been Jokers. As many artefacts were found on cold worlds as hot ones, and the dark side of the sun took on a new meaning in the far orbits. Sidewinders, Tarquins, The Pod, the two Evolutions of Seard . . . they all could have been the Jokers.

Somewhere was the Jokers World. It had been a legend so long that it was not open to doubt. There, waiting, were the secrets of the Towers, the machines that made the Chain Stars, the frictionless bearing, the meaning of the universe.

The pinpoint junctions cast a pale light along the tunnel. Dom hurried forward, darting around a small wheeled robot that was inspecting a junction box.

They broke into a cavern, and Hrsh-Hgn stared up at the shadowy machine that loomed above them. He nudged Dom and pointed upwards.

'Do you know what that iss?' he hissed.

'It's a matrix engine,' said Dom. 'Warship size. The Bank's got his own ships, hasn't he?'

'I believe not.'

A wheeled robot braked in front of them. It extended a padded arm and pushed at them, ineffectually. They hurried on.

The tunnel led into a cavern off the main hall. It was thronged, as usual. The entrance to the ship park was on the far side.

They split up. Dom dodged among the groups, keeping an eye open for Widdershins robots. Hrsh-Hgn loped stiffly in what passed on Phnobis for a conspiratorial walk.

Dom was halfway across the glittering floor when he glimpsed Joan entering the hall, with three security robots on either side of her.

She seemed to dwarf them. She looked determined.

He ducked back and a hand gripped his shoulder. He spun round.

The man was smiling. The smile looked awkward on that face.

He saw the blue robe and the heavy gold band around the neck, and Dom remembered. He tried to back away, but the hand followed him. It was the man at the party.

'Please don't be afraid.' Dom squirmed under the grip. There was a flurry and the hand flew off his shoulder, Ig's needle-sharp teeth buried in a finger. But the man did not scream, although his faced paled. Dom stepped back into the embrace of a robot.

He took off. Strictly speaking, flying within the bounds of the Bank was illegal. He just hoped the Bank would not interfere.

The sandals were built for one, though they could operate in strong gravity fields. Below them two other robots were staring vacantly upwards, and across the floor two more had Hrsh-Hgn cornered.

There was an eerie calmness about the vertical flight. The roar of the crowd dropped away, leaving only the underlying thunder of the Bank. He looked into the robot's multifaceted eyes, which mirrored the corona effects on the surrounding pillars.

'You're a Class Two, aren't you?' he asked.

'That is so, sir,' said the robot.

'Are you equipped with any motivation towards personal safety?'

'No, sir.' The robot glanced down. 'Unfortunately.'

Dom kicked his heels together and went into a dive. Thirty yards above the floor he twisted and felt his shirt tear as the robot lost its grip. It continued to fall in a long arc which ended abruptly in a glistening pillar of germanium. There was a flash and a rain of hot droplets.

Two other robots were rising from the floor on lift belts. Dom shot upwards, giddily, watching the distant roof grow. It was specked with black dots. It was only when he drew nearer he saw that they were caves.

It was hot near the roof. The air roared into the caves and Dom flew with it, because there was nothing else to do. He swam in a torrent of warm air, which buffeted him as it thundered along a tunnel.

And over Hell.

He was able to look down for a few seconds before the Hell-wind caught him.

He had been carried out into a mile-wide ventilation shaft. Between his feet the walls narrowed down, mile after mile, lit at the end by a white-hot eye. Thunder rolled around the shaft. It sounded like the churning of distant mighty engines. And the heat was palpable, tangible, like a hammer. It caught him like a leaf and fired him like a bullet.

Dom tumbled out of the shaft and towards the stars, balanced on a gout of superheated air. Night was all around him. In one direction – up and down had lost their usual positions – was the web of cold stars. In the other there was just one, a hungry red eye with a white pupil.

It seemed to drift away. Smoke from the grav sandals streamed around him. Something else had caught him, something which was always waiting, beyond the light. He wondered, dimly, through layers of pain, what it was touched him almost pleasantly, freezing his breath in his throat and making a pattern of crystals across his blistered skin.

Widdershine are agile. Among the fishers the awkward, the clumsy soon lost all their lives, and something of this rubbed off among the Board families. And so Dom landed on his feet, hard, and fell forward into the snow.

He knew what snow was. Keja had sent him a preserved snowflake from one of the colder regions of Laoth, and it looked something like the thin frost that briefly mantled the polar swamps of his own world, in the coldest winters. But Keja had not said that there could be so many of them.

7

On Widdershins it was Hogswatchnight, which coincided with Small Gods in the greater Sadhimist calendar. It usually meant a larger klatch meeting, or a number of klatches would join together in celebration, but by midnight every group would be split so that each member watched the dawn alone. But as the older Sadhimist averred darkly, one was never fully alone at Hogswatch. By dawn, perhaps, some men would be poets or prophets or even be possessed of a new minor talent, like being able to play the thumb-flute. And one or two would be mad.

The ground underneath him was warm.

Dom lay in the tepid water for some time before he realized it. He was spreadeagled in a large, steaming puddle. Beyond it the snowdrifts started.

He heard the distant air scream. Something

hurled across the stars, trailing a sonic boom. It turned in a tight, gravity-squeezing circle, returned slowly and slammed neatly to a halt on the edge of the puddle. Except that it didn't work. The water was freezing again. The ship danced drunkenly between the drifts and returned, a few minutes later, under very low power.

Isaac opened the hatch.

'Now, are we getting out of this place or aren't we?' he cried.

'Mint soda, chief?'

Dom took the glass. Ice tinkled. Frost was forming on the sides. It tasted like a dive into a snowbank.

There was fresh green skin on his arms and legs and the back of his neck, where the googoo had reformed itself to his body memory.

Isaac pressed the memory button on the ship's workshop and slid the soles back on the sandals. He tossed them across to Dom.

'Short-circuited in the heat,' he said. 'They should be okay now.'

Dom stared out at the starlit surface of the Bank. The warm pool had already frozen over. It made a glittering circle in the snow. He had been lucky, at that. On the sunny side of the Bank water boiled in the shade. He raised the Bank on the ship's radio.

Hrsh-Hgn had been taken aboard the *Drunk*, destination unknown. The Bank knew nothing about the man with the gold collar, or the whereabouts of Ig. It had warmed the surface and sent Isaac out because – because deaths on the Bank were rare and he disliked the subsequent investigations.

Dom switched off, and drummed his fingers on the console. His face was reflected in the empty screen.

It was dark green, mottled with leaf-green, because body memory took no account of tanning. He was naked in the stable ship temperature. The memory of recent pain still showed in his eyes, but he was thinking of a man in a gold collar, a smiling man who had haunted his dreams.

'No one notices him,' he said out loud. 'He's just a face in the crowd. He's trying to kill me.'

Idly he picked up Korodore's gift. He'd already experimented with it, putting the memory sword through its repertoire, and now he watched as the atoms reprogrammed themselves. A twitch, and it was a needle sword . . . a short knife . . . a gun, that froze bullets out of atmospheric water and could fire them through steel hull metal . . . another gun, a sonic . . .

'I don't know how Grandmother chased me here,' he said. 'Though it is the logical place. But I know where the *Drunk* is heading now.'

'Widdershins?' asked Isaac.

'Band. She'll get the information out of Hrsh. I imagine she'll threaten him with repatriation to Phnobis.'

'That doesn't sound like a threat, chief.'

'To a phnobe it is. If he goes back to Phnobis he'll be in swift conjunction with a ceremonial tshuri whatever happens. No, he'll talk.'

Isaac slipped into the pilot seat.

'You could go back to Widdershins. Your grandmother has your best interests at heart.'

'I've got to go on. I can't describe it, I just haven't got a choice. Do you understand?'

'No, boss. Band, then? I've calibrated the matrix computer. It should work.'

'You'd better believe it.'

He hefted the memory sword. If someone else was waiting at Band . . .

Glowing walls. Ghostly, half-melting visions. The miniature stars and claustrophobic feel of a ship in interspace. And the visions.

'Chel, what was that?'

'It looked like a dinosaur, boss. Striped.'

He fingered the collar at his neck, and showed no anger. Anger clouded the faculties, and so he lived in a state of constant disassociation. But sometimes he thought, not angry thoughts, but little cold statements about what he would do if the collar was removed.

What he would do to Asman, in particular. And to the misguided genius who invented the collar circuitry.

The door opened.

Asman looked up, and froze. Behind him the long room became silent, just for a second. It usually happened like this. And Asman would point the gun . . .

Asman pointed the gun, and nodded towards the three dice in their cup. The gun was a stripper, with every safety device removed and a hair trigger. He knew that Asman would fire by reflex action if necessary.

He threw three sixes.

'Again.' He threw three sixes.

'Again?' he asked mildly. Asman smiled weakly, got up and shook his hand.

'I'm sorry,' he said. 'You know how it is.'

'One day I'll make a mistake. Have you thought of that?'

'Ways, the day you make a mistake like that you won't be Ways any more, and you know I'll fire, because you'll be an imposter.'

Asman rounded the table and clapped him on the shoulder.

'You've been doing well,' he said.

'How else?'

Ways had seen his own specification, just once. He had been halfway down an inspection shaft at the time, one that was flooded with chlorine gas when not in official use, and gaining illegal access to personnel files was not official. He had never bothered to remember the precise purpose of his visit – it was just one of the many assignments that filtered down to him via Asman's office – but while the little inspection screen was warming up his specification had appeared among the random images. He had memorized it instantly, even through the chlorine haze.

It was a standard requisition for a Class Five robot, with certain important modifications concerning concealed weapons, communicators, and appearance. Designing a completely humanoid robot was twice as complex as building even a high-grade Class Five. It involved intricate machinery for tear ducts and the growth of facial hair – and, if the robot was designed as a spy and might be faced with every eventuality, an intriguing range of other equipment also . . .

But most of Ways' specifications had been in probability math. It took him some time to realize why. Class Five robots were legally human. They had been designed to be everything a man could be, and Ways had been designed to be lucky.

Asman led him to the mural that occupied one long wall of the large, low-ceilinged room. The room itself was featureless, as were the men tending the machines. It could have been the security room of any Board-run world. But there was something about the quality of the air, even of the light, that suggested an underground vault – Ways in fact sensed the layer upon layer of shielding around him – and there was something in the confident, unthinking way that the Earthman Asman moved that suggested in which planetary crust the room was buried.

The mural was a brightly lit tangle of coloured lines, circles and blocks of p-math, that shifted slightly as he watched.

'You've done well,' Asman said again. 'He's moved along the right equation.'

'As to that, how do I know? I just keep trying to kill him, just like the others. Do you want me to try on Band?'

'No, your next point of intervention should be . . .' he glanced along the rainbow lines '. . . oh, not till he visits those Creap. We've got contingency plans for that. It's all in the equation, anyway. We'll be hot on their heels then, if they have heels. The math says so. One more intervention when he gets to Laoth and we'll be in the Joker universe.'

Ways blinked slowly. 'Is this information I need to know?'

Asman returned his gaze. 'What do you mean by that?'

'Look,' said Ways, sitting down, 'you made

me. Not you, precisely, but someone on Laoth or Lunar. They made me. I'm a robot.'

'That's not held against you. If we were Creap we'd have simply bred up a Creap with the required characteristics, in some vat. But you can't wamp up a man, so you . . .'

'Okay, but I'm a robot, even if I'm a special one. I've got everything from toenails to offensive underarm odours, but that's all faked. So what does it matter what a robot knows?'

'You've made your point. Now, are you interested?' Asman was growing impatient.

'Certainly. Why doesn't he die when I kill him?'

'The universe alters.'

Shoot a man from point-blank range, so that your beam dislodges every organic molecule from hair to feet. All the rules postulate an outcome of, say, a monomolecular mist, a few zips and geegaws on the floor, and a faint smell of burning. But there is always the outside chance. The stripper goes imperceptibly out of sync. Or you hallucinated that you pressed the stud, and didn't. In a shifting universe there is no such thing as a rock-hard certainty, only a local eddy in the stream of total randomness. Just occasionally the coin comes down on its edge, or doesn't come down at all.

'Dom Sabalos is likely to discover Jokers World in . . .' Asman glanced at the far end of the mural . . . 'twenty days, Standard. We can't stop him.

He's our first failure out of, oh, it must be several thousand now.'

'Two thousand three hundred and nine,' said Ways. 'I killed them.'

'They all had the right life equations. Any one of them could have made the discovery. His father, for example.'

'And now it isn't working,' said Ways. 'We've found some history we can't change. And we're suspected, you know. Look at young Sabalos. All those precautions, on such a harmless world. The Sabaloses are a popular family. After the death of his father they must have felt that he was in danger, too, and not from a Widdershine. I don't think he was even told about the Jokers until he was out of childhood. Another thing. We are driving him to Jokers World.'

Asman rubbed his hands thoughtfully.

'We have considered that,' he said.

'If we hadn't made the attempts he'd probably still be on Widdershins. Instead he's flying around with a robot and a Joker expert – quite a good one, too, from what I've heard.'

Asman nodded. 'Of course, one doesn't have to travel to discover,' he said. 'However, what you say is true. We have been working on a contingency plan. If all else fails we can follow him.'

There was a heavy silence. Ways said quietly: 'To the dark side of the sun?'

'If there is no alternative, yes. Wherever it may

be. According to our latest equations, that is what we will do.'

'So you are preparing for it?'

'Oh yes. Sometimes, robot, I get the horrible feeling that we live in a big ever-repeating circle where we do things because it is predicted that we will do things – all effect and no cause. We'll go, anyway, and we will go armed.'

Ways looked at the man, and around the long low room. For a moment he considered the possibility of a universe caught in a circle of predict-and-effect, the ultimate closed circuit, and wondered if the inhabitants would realize what they had done.

'That's not enough,' he said. 'Why isn't he dying?'

Asman shrugged. 'Would you believe the Jokers alter the universe just so that he can remain alive? That's the current favourite. Maybe they want him to discover their world. Maybe – and this one is our prime hypothesis – they are waiting to be discovered. Perhaps this is all necessary to jog him through slightly differing alternate universes into the one where the Jokers exist. That's an outsider, but worth considering.'

Ways was silent.

'That gives you something to think about, eh?'

He nodded. Then he pulled aside his cloak and made a few passes over his chest. A partition slid back and he extracted a small cage, hastily soldered together from power wire. Inside, a small rat-like creature, six-legged and pink, gyrated and yowled, spitting at Asman.

'His pet,' said Asman.

'I expect you knew about this,' said the robot.

'It's on the board,' he admitted. 'We didn't bother to go into details. So this is Ig. Strange little thing, isn't he?'

'It's an it,' said Ways. 'Ask me to tell you how they breed, and I'll answer loudly and with gusto. They eat everything, even artificial epidermi as it turns out.' He held up a finger, bitten to the alloy. 'I'm the latest expert on them. Widdershine fishers say they're the souls of drowned men, to which they may bear some resemblance. They're the third largest air-breathing creature that the planet has produced. Phnobes think they're lucky, and the fishers say that if one makes a pet of you it means death will never be lethal. It could be they have a rudimentary psychic sense, like dogs or Third Eye dragons. It's difficult to see why, since they have no natural enemies and they're something of a planetary totem. The bomb should be planted inside the ribcage, I suggest.'

'Bomb?'

'You plan that Dom should be killed after we've discovered the position of Jokers World. You didn't tell me that, by the way. I suggest that this is what you have in mind. This thing sticks to him. I can see it gets back to him.'

Asman covered the cage. 'As a matter of fact, we have considered something like that. Fine,' he added, with just a hint of nervousness.

While an underling spirited the cage away he added: 'You enjoy food?'

'To some extent the calories are a useful power supplement, as you know.'

So they went to The Dark Side of The Sun, a low mock-phnobic building built on and merging with the sand hills between the Joker Institute and the Minnesota Sea. It was one of many. The Institute had attracted a sizeable town, based on the Joker Industry, a limited amount of tourism and alien visitors. Most of the Earth tourists came to see the aliens and feel cosmospolitan, and the management of the Dark Side tried to cater for this. The walls were decorated with imaginative hologram murals – Creapii sun rafts drifting across Lutyen 789–6, a drosk eight-unit at a funeral feast, grim-faced gardeners fighting a rogue tree on Eggplant, Spooners doing nothing very comprehensible on an unknown ice world.

There were sculptures, too. The phnobic display was unconvincing and probably a fake, although the snow sculpture by an unnamed Tka-peninsular drosk was almost certainly genuine, and so was the . . . thing, difficult to describe or even to comprehend, that spun slowly around the ceiling, occasionally bumping the walls. The floor covering was an alive and semi-sapient Bowdler, on the payroll, and the serving robots were genuine Laothans. The Dark Side was in fact well patronized by the more adaptable aliens, who appreciated its cooking and prized its uniquely Earth ambience.

A copperplate motto on the menu read: 'We Serve Anything.'

'There's the story about the drosk chieftain who walked in here and demanded her grand-mother's brains on toast,' began Asman, as they sat down.

'And they said sorry, we've run out of bread,' said Ways. 'That story gets around, I last heard it on 'Nova. I'll have what you have, if it's starchy.'

'We'll eat Pineal, I think. Fast-Luck Couscous.'

Behind Asman's head was another mural, and since it was a special one it made the table rather special too, which was why Asman had been shown there with a great deal of ceremony. The Director of the Institute was a big attraction.

The mural depicted a score or so of the more recognizable races grouped in an obviously sub-ordinate position around a throne, on which sat a man. He was human, though attenuated like a Pineal, and wore a harlequin suit and a cap and bells. He was smiling. Behind him was a sun, one hemisphere in shadow and the other appearing from this angle only as a thin crescent.

'Any special reason why the Joker is human?' Ways asked. He took a handful from the steaming pot, kneaded it expertly and swallowed it whole.

'Not really. "Joker" is a purely human translation. If you are going to portray one in representational terms, he's got to be human or humanoid,' said Asman. He grinned sidelong at Ways. 'Do you agree with the rest of the symbology?'

'The Joker as Lord of Creation? It chimes in with the idea that they gave life a hand in these parts. There's something about the expression that suggests it wasn't from altruistic motives. Slave races?'

'Possibly. Humanity – and I mean real humanity, the sort that ends at Lunar – cannot afford to meet the Jokers whatever they may be. They've had at least five million years' start on us. More important, they had the galaxy to themselves. They didn't have to learn how to get along. That's why we run the search. We can't afford to let them find us first.'

'You assume they're still alive, then?'

'What could have killed them? What sort of gods – or devils – have they become? I think they are hiding. And waiting.'

'What will happen to me?' asked Ways quietly. Asman looked startled, then assumed a blank expression just a moment too soon.

'You want to leave the Institute?'

'This,' Ways fingered the gold collar, 'is the only thing that binds me. Yes, I want to leave. I know how much I cost. That's the advantage of being a robot, there are no big unanswered questions. I know my worth, I know why I was created. I'll repay every pico-standard. But you can keep the humanoid trappings. I won't need them.'

He somersaulted backwards, smashing the chair and landing with his legs folding under him ready for the next leap. It took him across a table and towards a running man, who fell with Ways' alloy hands gripping his wrists just hard enough to agonize. A small sonic gun bounced on the carpet, which writhed.

The robot's arm flicked out in a quicksilver motion and a finger stabbed at the man's neck. He collapsed, neatly and without a sound. Ways bowed an apology to a diner from Whole Erse, who was gazing at his shattered meal, and strode back to Asman's table.

'I'm sorry about that,' said the Director. 'Assassins are a hazard in my line.'

'He was too noisy focusing that sonic,' said Ways. 'I hope you were given due notice?'

'Oh yes, three days and a regular United Spies contract. But I didn't expect anything here, the management have an arrangement. I trust they'll register a complaint.'

'Did the contract say who was behind him?'

'No. It was the old standard Projectile or

146

Energy Discharge form. I think it was one of my
. . . but that's my problem. Thank you.'

Two Institute security guards walked in
tactfully and removed the body. Ways scanned
the room. Two minor Board of Earth officials
were complaining to the head waiter, but
the non-Earth diners had settled down again.
Some of them may have thought it was part of
the floor show. During the Starveall ceremony
on Whole Erse there were dancers who . . . Ways
clamped down on the unwanted information,
and glanced at two diners half-hidden by
the luxuriant growth of a dormant Eggplant
pinpointer-plant, a large, scarred man in plain
but well-grown clothes, and an antique serving
robot. They hadn't even looked up during the
assassination attempt. They were playing some
game with small robots on a chequerboard.

He turned to Asman.

'I will leave,' he said. 'After this last affair
is concluded, I will sever my connection with
the Institute under the seventeenth sub Law of
Robotics. Thank you for the meal. It was most
energizing. Good evening.'

When the robot had gone Asman sat back
and gazed at the far wall thoughtfully. There
was a chiming in his inner ear, followed by a
familiar voice. Two familiar voices. Except that
they weren't voices, they circumnavigated the
tedious aural processes and arrived fresh at his
consciousness.

'Interesting.'

'Possibly so, but I suggest you dissassemble him immediately,' said the second voice.

Asman thought: 'Mr Chairman, how many are sitting in on this.'

'Just myself and the Lady Ladkin. This is by no means a formal Board meeting. We watched the proceedings with interest, though without, I fear, unanimity as to conclusion,' came the first voice.

Asman nodded to the waiter and strolled out into the night, taking a winding, sand-strewn path back to the Institute.

'Ways will go through with it,' he thought.

Lady Ladkin's tone was petulant. 'Why do we need to bother with this robot? I know a dozen people who have the required combination of loyalty and mayhem.'

'My Lady, apart from the prediction that a robot such as Ways would be used by us,' he hurried on quickly before she could interrupt, 'he has certainly proved himself in similar assassinations. He initiated the Novean Board debacle, for example. My Lord Pan, may I be heard?'

'Go ahead,' came the rumbling tone of the Chairman. 'At present I am attending the première concert of the Third Eye Tactile Orchestra. They lack sparkle.'

'My Lord, and my Lady, I arranged this evening as you wished, at some risk to myself.

The assassin might have succeeded. US were understanding about my request, but I had to sign a waiver, and I dare say they put their best man in. Now, you know we monitor the robot. He hates the Institute, of course, and to some extent he had sympathy for Sabalos—'

'As indeed I do also,' said Pan, and this time Asman caught the distant echo of the orchestra. 'I believe I met him once. His grandmother and myself were once very friendly. Old, she must be now, very old. A fine woman. Ah, we have heard the chimes at twenty-four hundred hours, Master Shallow.'

'We must consider the boy as an instrument, my Lord,' thought Asman patiently, picking his way between the dunes. 'Ways feels sorry for him, but I think I have proved to your satisfaction that in actions he has no choice but to be loyal to us. As he himself said, he is a robot, and even a Class Five can be built with certain imperatives.'

'That collar . . .' began Lady Ladkin.

'It will activate itself in the unlikely event of Ways taking any but the prescribed course,' thought Asman soothingly.

She grumbled and was silent.

'May I go ahead, then?'

There was another echo of music. 'This is derivative stuff. Oh, yes, go ahead. We are secure in our predictions, aren't we? I am not altogether happy about booby-trapping his pet

149

– I myself have several cats, of which I am fond – but we must be practical. Proceed. I look forward to receiving your full report.'

Asman was suddenly alone among the dunes.

Dom awoke. For a while he floated, piecing his thoughts together. Then he pushed himself forward with his toe and drifted across the cabin.

Day had come to this side of the Band, although the evening terminator was visibly racing across the planet, and the Band-on-Band was fully visible.

It was a 3,000-mile-wide equatorial strip of land that girdled the fat world like a corset. Even up here Band appeared to revolve so fast for a planet that an imaginative observer half-expected to hear a background hum. It bulged. The Band was a grey-brown strip of mountain, one continuous 25,000-mile range, edged by two ribbons of blue-green grassland. They were bounded by two strips of darker sea, which reached up to the squashed poles and the white ice.

'It's explainable in terms of continental drift, high rotation and ancient vulcanism, boss,' said Isaac, looking up from the autochef. 'Or didn't you want to know?'

'It must be a hell of a place to live on,' said Dom, 'what with the sun scooting across the sky and all.'

'The sundogs like it.'

Dom nodded. It was their world. They had evolved on Eggplant, but 600 years ago had accepted a cash grant and the deeds of Band in exchange for vacant possession. Sundogs were nice, but dangerous to live with in the laying season. So far Dom's telescopic survey had revealed nothing but herds of sundog pups which could be seen from space as large dots at one end of thousand-mile-long swathes grazed through Band's ubiquitous sweetgrass.

There were two narrow strips of marshland, and rivers in the mountains. There was one small lake. There was absolutely no sign of any habitation.

Dom had checked on the world. The Creapii-backed Wildlife Preservation Fund ran a small robotic observation station on the planet, as part of a treaty which also forbade unauthorized landings. The Fund headquarters said that there had been suggestions that a being known as Chatogaster was a pre-Sundog inhabitant, although the planet had a meagre selection of vegetation and no animal life at all. No, no signs of sapience had been exhibited by the vegetation. Band had no higher life of its own, which was why the sundogs selected it. Chatogaster was considered to be a sundog legend, or a planetary spirit. No, there had been no recent landings. Very rarely a ship had to put in under the emergency clause, but the robot station was equipped to handle that. Thank you for your enquiry.

Such sundogs as Dom had been able to raise had refused to discuss the subject. There were a lot of them orbiting the planet.

As Band spun below the ship they came yet again into radio range of *Drunk With Infinity*. The set crackled and Joan spoke.

'Still not coming down, Dom? Be reasonable. I don't think you are being astute about this at all.'

Her voice made a background as Dom unshipped the telescope again and peered down at the planet.

Seen from several thousand miles up the *Drunk* was a squat blob at one end of a long shadow which, Dom swore, shortened as he watched it. It stood in the middle of the rolling continental plain of grass, midway between mountains and sea and only ten miles or so from the solitary lake. Here and there around the ship the yellow light glinted off metal. Robots.

'Anyway, you've been up there for hours. You will have to land soon for air, and I happen to know that by now you can't have enough fuel to take off again. Be reasonable. I am not your enemy. Please come back to Widdershins: you don't know the danger you're in.'

Dom looked across at the fuel tell-tale for the hundredth time. She was quite right.

In desperation he turned to the *One Jump's*

planetary guide, which he had found in its library among some suggestive books on economics.

'It is a sparsely furnished world, though beautiful from space,' he read. 'It is the nearest thing a rock world can become to looking like a gas giant. Band was discovered and claimed by the Creapii in B.S. 5,356, but is leased by the sundogs for the purpose of raising their pups. Unauthorized landing is banned – the planet's name is hence very apt – except in cases of emergency. Even then, for obvious reasons, landings should not be made in the late orbital spring.'

Obvious reasons, thought Dom. He was pre-pared to bet that it was late spring down there. But Hrsh-Hgn was down there too, and so was a non-existent being called Chatogaster.

'Well,' he said. 'This is what we'll do . . .'

'They are landing, ma'am.'

Joan flounced across the cabin and swept the robot from the control seat.

The screen showed a thin line raking over the planet. It arched down and presently the vision screens showed the *One Jump*, skimming low over the plains with an impressive show of stunt flying.

'A gesture of defiance. A Sabalos to the core,' she said proudly. 'There's no shame in

giving in when you've no alternative whatso-
ever.'

The small ship swung round and landed a
mile away from the *Drunk*, scattering a herd of
giant sundog pups which trundled off clumsily,
keening.

'Eight, Three, go off and escort him in.'

Two of the robots outside broke away and
lurched off through the knee-high grass.

'That's settled, then,' said Joan. She swung
round in her seat and sent down to the butler's
pantry for a jug of bitter Pineal wine. The only
other occupant of the cabin gazed at her mourn-
fully.

There were three sexes on Phnobis, but
equally there were two other distinctions among
phnobes: those who lived on Phnobis, and those
who did not. The two were not interchangeable.
There were no return tickets. Phnobic religion
was adamant that the universe ended at the
unbroken cloud layer, and returning phnobes
were bad for business – hence, by a roundabout
route, the big, artificially overcast *burukus* on
every other world.

'It appears that I won't have to send you back
after all.'

'For thiss relief much thankss.' Hrsh-Hgn
grimaced and massaged his long ribcage. 'Your
robots are ungentle, madam.'

'They used little more than the necessary
minimum of force, I'm sure.' She leaned

forward. 'Tell me – purely out of interest – what precisely happens to returning phnobes?'

'The shipss have to land in a ssacred area. Alighting phnobes are dispatched with a knife, it is ssaid. It iss not reasonable. I send all my salary to the sacred coffers, ass you know. Ah, well. As the ssaying runs, Frskss Shhs Ghs Ghnng-ghngss.'

Joan raised her eyebrows. 'Indeed? Hrskss-gng, my dear fellow, and many of them.'

Hrsh-Hgn blushed grey. 'Your pardon, madam, I did not realize you sspoke . . .' He looked at her with new respect.

'I don't. But there are some words one learns on even passing acquaintance with a language. To an Earth-human woman it's a compliment, actually, if somewhat direct.'

She turned back to the screen.

Robots Eight and Three plodded up to the ship, from which came the strains of the Widder-shine ballad 'Do You Take Me for a Silly?' played inexpertly on a thumb-organ. A puppy lumbered away as they approached.

The hatch was open. Three stepped in.

Isaac regarded him amiably.

'I perceive the human is not here,' said Three.

'That is correct,' said Isaac.

Three eyed him warily. Finally he intoned: 'I am a Class Three robot. I ask you to remain here while I seek instruction.'

'I, on the other hand, am a Class Five robot,

with additional Man-Friday subcircuitry,' said Isaac pleasantly.

Three's left eyeball twitched. Isaac had picked up a spanner.

'I perceive a possibility of an immediate chronological sequence of events which includes a violence,' said Three. He stepped back. 'I express preference for a chronological sequence of events which precludes a violence.'

Eight poked his head round the hatchway and added, 'I too express a preference for a chronological sequence of events which precludes a violence.'

Isaac hefted the spanner thoughtfully. 'You are advanced fellows for Class Threes. There's just you and me here, and we none of us are non-metallic humans. Do you intend to molest me?'

'Our orders are to escort the contents of this machine to our mistress,' said Three. He was watching the spanner.

'You could disobey.'

'Class Fives may disobey. Class Fours may disobey in special circumstances. We are not Class Fives. We are not Class Fours. It is a matter for regret.'

'Then I will temporarily disable you,' said Isaac firmly.

'Although you are more intelligent than myself I will resist,' said Three. He shifted uneasily.

'We will resort to violence on the count of three,' said Isaac. 'One. Two.'

The spanner clonked against Three's cut-out button. 'Three,' said Isaac, and turned to Eight who was staring at his fallen comrade with a perplexed air.

'I perceive an illogical sequence of events which included a violence,' he said. Isaac hit him.

It took him some time to strip himself of his facemask and streamlining and transfer a large plastic 'Three' to his naked chestplate. Then he set off for the other ship with the exultant air of one who hears distant bugles.

He reached the stateroom without molestation. Joan looked up.

'You took your time,' she said. 'Where are they? And where is Eight?'

'There was a recent chronological sequence of events that included a violence,' said Isaac. In one movement he picked Hrsh-Hgn bodily off his stool, slung him over his shoulder and fled. He skidded through the airlock a moment before it hissed shut.

Outside the ship he stood the phnobe upright and pointed eastwards. 'Run. There's a lake. I will join you shortly,' he added. 'At the moment I perceive an imminent number of violences.'

Twenty guard robots wheeled as one on Joan's amplified command and ran towards him.

He stood his ground, which seemed to worry

them. To the first who approached he said: 'Are you Class Threes, all of you?'

The robot called Twelve said: 'Some of us are Class Two robots, but most of us are Class Three robots. I am a Class Three robot myself.'

Isaac looked at the sky. He felt very happy. It was very wrong of him.

'Correction,' he said. 'As of now you are all recumbent waterfowl of the genus *Scipidae*.'

Twelve paused. 'I am a Class Three robot myself,' he said uncertainly.

'Correction,' said Isaac. 'I repeat, you are all sitting ducks. Now, I am going to count three . . .'

He walked forward, and his atomic heart sang a lyrical hymn of superior intelligence.

Dom dropped from the speeding yacht before it entered visor range of the *Drunk* and spun giddily in its slipstream until the sandals steadied him. He drifted down to a few feet above the close-cropped plain and set off at a fast skimming trot eastwards.

He skated for ten minutes over the sweetgrass which, apart from a variety of weeds, several lichens and some seaweeds, was the only vegetation on the planet. On Band nature had stuck to a few tried and tested lines.

Several times he passed flocks of puppies, large ungainly creatures that from space appeared to drift like clouds over the continent. Here and there a larger one moped apart from the main herds, squatting on its bloated rump and staring at the sky with mournful eyes, with a skin the unhealthy pallor of a sundog soon to undergo puberty. Usually they smelt of fermenting sweetgrass.

When Dom passed one it gave a tired whine and staggered a few yards on its stumpy legs before taking up its yearning position once more.

82 Erandini rose quickly towards noon.

The robot station was on the far side of the lake, probably because the lake was one of the few marker points on Band. Dom had decided to try there. Chatogaster had to be somewhere.

He paused for a sip of water and the cold, cooked leg of some flightless bird, courtesy of the autochef. The air was warm and springlike. The eternal sound of chewing as the sunpups grazed their way relentlessly round the world made a pleasant background.

The air in front of Dom crackled. A small metal sphere whirred to a halt and hung on its antigravs. It eyed Dom and extruded a mouthpiece.

'I perceive you are an ambulatory intelligence, type B,' it said. 'Crackdown in this area is forecast in ten minutes. Don your protective clothing or seek chthonic safety.'

It rose and hurtled northwards screaming, 'Crackdown! Crackdown! Beware of the eggs!'

'Oi!' bellowed Dom. The sphere returned, fast. 'Well?'

'I don't understand.'

The sphere considered this. 'I am a Class One mind,' it said finally. 'I will seek reinstruction.'

It disappeared again. A distant cry of, 'Beware of the eggs,' marked its going.

Dom watched it and shrugged. He looked round warily, drawing the memory sword from his belt. Most of the sunpups, in fact all except the sky watchers, were lying down and peacefully chewing. It looked idyllic.

Half a world away, and above the glowing surf of the atmosphere, Crackdown was beginning. The sundogs were in orbit. They had laid their eggs. Now incubation began its final stage.

The leading egg roared through the superheated air, the forward heatshell leaving a searing trail. Finally it cracked at the pointed end and the first parachute burst open. Around the egg the sky filled with other blossoming white membranes.

The first egg for ten years hit the ground a hundred miles to the north of Dom. The overheated shell burst into a thousand fragments that scythed the grass for yards around . . .

The second landed to the west of the lake. The shell exploded violently and red-hot shards showered over a herd of puppies who, in response to an ancient instinct, were lying down safely with their padded forepaws over their heads.

From behind one came a Phnobic curseword.

8

Dom bounced across the grass. Shell was flying all around him. There was already a long burn across one shoulder where a shard had narrowly missed taking off his head.

The ground in front suddenly dipped, and the lake stretched out in front of him. It was big. It was also cold, and probably safe. He gunned his sandals and took a standing jump.

The dive was from a height, and ended a long way down. He turned in a shoal of bubbles and struck out for surface. His ears rang. He was still sinking.

Unbelieving, he felt his feet touch the lake bottom. Goggle-eyed, he felt the water round his feet warm up as his sandals tried uselessly to push him to the surface. Drowning, he breathed a chestful of water.

He was several fathoms down. He was breathing water. He took another breath, and tried not to think about it.

The water is saturated with oxygen. It will sustain you.

A large silver fish stared at him, and was away with a flick of its tail. Something like a ten-legged crab scuttled over his feet.

Do not be frightened.

It was a sound. Something was talking to him.

'You are Chatogaster, then.' He peered into the murky water. 'They looked for an aquatic creature, but they looked in the seas. I can't see you.'

I am here. You are thinking in the wrong terms.

The water shone with stars. They winked on above, around, below. He could still feel the water eddy around him, but all other senses told him that he was standing and breathing in interstellar space. Deep space. The centre of a star cluster.

No, the hub of the galaxy.

'It's an illusion.'

No, it's a memory. Watch.

At the hub of the galaxy where the stars rubbed shoulders and interstellar distances were measured in light weeks a planet was bathed in the violent light of a hundred suns. It was made of water.

At the centre it was Water IV, the third strangest substance in the universe, and the surface boiled. Dom watched the facts form in his mind with the inexorable growth of crystals.

For a few thousand years the planet glooped and woobled its watery path between the stars, trailing behind it across the galactic sky a shimmering rainbow of steam that photon pressure sculptured into vast ghosts. Then it exploded.

Dom found himself ducking. A churning droplet of water, a whole sea, left the damp explosion and passed him, steaming, on its way to the galactic rim.

And he knew with a second-hand certainty that the hot wet world had produced life. It was a life that knew nothing of Jokers. In the hot water improbable compounds had formed unlikely molecules, had . . .

'You are the lake,' he said.

I am. How is my old friend the Bank?

'He was fine a few days ago,' said Dom. 'Uh . . . do you shun publicity?'

Not at all, but I like my privacy. The Bank was the only other lifeform extant when I arrived here. The sundogs know me. But I help them, I take care of their pups, and they are reticent about me.

'Take care of their pups? You must be telepathic.'

Not as you would understand it. But most creatures are largely water, and I am wholly water. They drink of me, and I become part of them – as I am part of you. Osmosis, you see. Don't let it offend you.

'I won't,' said Dom. He kicked a cloud of mud from the lake bottom, and tried to convince himself.

Eight of our days ago the Bank sent me a messenger. The Bank is rock, I am water. We have an understanding.

Dom smiled. 'Isn't there some story about a sapient sun out towards galactic north?' he asked.

Yes, it is true. He is strange. We are instituting a search for an intelligent gas cloud now, to complete the elemental quartet. However, the Bank told me that he was sending a person to aid my extension programme.

'He didn't say that to me – I was told you could help me find Jokers World,' said Dom.

Maybe we can help one another.

'What do you know about the Jokers?'

Nothing. Knowledge is not my province. My province is . . .

There was no precise word for it. A series of images flashed across Dom's mind as Chatogaster tried to explain. Intuition was too coarse a term; there was something in it of a leaf's knowledge of how a tree grows; there was something warm, dreamy, arcane . . .

May I rifle your memory? I shall need to. Thank you. You may experience a dreamlike sensation, however, I will leave your mind as I would wish to find it.

Later the lake said: *Generally speaking there is no dark side to a sun. Let us start with the Joker towers. Their casing at least is probably a giant molecule. Their use is not known, although they absorb power and appear to yield none. I feel bound to say that there is no apparent reason for their existence, any more than there is for a man, for example.*

It would seem that this assassin is out to prevent you from discovering this World. He may in fact be hastening your discovery by forcing you along paths you might not otherwise take.

Let us consider the Jokers themselves. That they existed cannot be doubted. They have left artefacts, the greatest of which are the Chain Stars, which proves they had power and perhaps bravado; they left the Centre of the Universe on Wolf, which suggests they had an understanding of the underlying truisms of Totality; and they left the Tomorrow Strata on Third Eye, which I believe means they at least experimented with time travel. There is a fundamental mistake, though, in assuming that the Jokers are the sum of their creations. These may have been toys, relics of the Jokers' youth. Astronomical evidence suggests that if they evolved on a world it may well be dead and gone by now. The fact that Jokers World has not been found within the 'life-bubble' does not lead me to believe it is hidden. I find I believe it is not there. It must be obvious that 'the dark side of the sun' is an idea rather than a place.

'It had crossed my mind,' admitted Dom. He was sitting in the ooze, watching the light dance on the surface overhead. 'Is it a poetic image?'

Poetry is the highest art. The Jokers must have achieved it.

Dom sighed. 'I had an idea at the start that it

166

was just a matter of finding some cute explanation like – well, like Hrsh-Hgn's.'

That is in fact very poetic, and quite possible. But it . . .

Another lapse into intranslatability. An itch; a sense of wrongness, traditionally embodied in the almost physical pain some people experienced in seeing a picture hung crooked and being unable to right it; a feeling of discord.

That would make them like Creapii. Environment conditions the mind, and the Jokers did not think like Creapii. However, the Creapii are indubitably the most advanced race at present. I suggest you study them. In the Creapii is a clue to the Jokers.

'So I won't discover a world.'

I did not say so. But the idea is more important. Do you not say 'the world of the common wasp', or 'the world of the poet'? They are worlds, and only incidentally include some reference to a physical reality like a planet.

'I think I see,' said Dom, getting up. 'The world of the Jokers may be just a way of looking at the universe?'

Precisely.

'I shall visit the Creapii.' He tried to remember. 'I think the High-Degrees have just opened a study raft on the Chain Stars, haven't they?'

So I understand. Since the High-Degrees represent the most advanced Creapii and specialize in the study of other lifeforms your choice of destination is a good one.

Dom prepared to swim to the surface, but stopped. 'There was something you wanted me to do?'

It is a great favour. You are Chairman of Widdershins, a world largely composed of water?

'On the surface, yes. Over ninety per cent, including the marshes.'

I would like to emigrate.

Chatogaster explained. Band was a pleasant world, but lacked stimulation. He could communicate with the liquid content of sundogs who had as pups drunk from the lake, and hence through their own telepathy – which was no more than a by-function of their massive brains – learn from the minds of travellers. But Chatogaster wanted to spread out. He needed no ship. If Dom could take the little container that had held his drinking water, and let it be filled, enough of Chatogaster could be taken to Widdershins to let the great Tethys ocean become Chatogaster as well. He was persuasive.

I could take care of your fish, and police your sea-lanes. I could provide surf with the muscles of the tide, and an inspiration for your poets. Who drinks of me drinks of the well of the universe. Please.

Dom hesitated, and the lake saw why.

I have no power. I may aid, but I cannot fight. What should I want with conquests? I am . . .

Untranslatable, but images of a mind rather than a force; an idea formed in water rather than a creature; a certainty that the lake was speaking

– not the truth, because that suggested it could lie, and Chatogaster could not lie . . .

'I may be overruled by the Board but,' he opened the little bottle that had been in his carryall, 'step right in.' An air bubble escaped from the bottle.

Thank you.

A kick carried Dom easily to the surface. He broke water and struck out for the shore.

Crackdown appeared to have ended. One or two eggs spiralled down as he scrambled up the slope, but they exploded a long way off in the south. A few damp pups, no bigger than a man, were taking their first shaky steps.

Here and there older pups were baying at the sky, long snouts pointing trembling at the clouds. The reddish hair on their cone-shaped bodies was sleeked down. One near to the lake was shuddering.

'Pssst!'

Hrsh-Hgn and a robot with a large Three on its chestplate leapt out of the grass. Without pausing in their stride they each grabbed him by an elbow and the three of them tumbled back towards the lake.

The air began to smell of methane, a fruity foul smell that caught in Dom's throat.

'Hrsh! Isaac got you, then? What's happened to Isaac? *You're* Isaac? What happened?'

The robot was half covered in soot, and there were superficial metal runs down one arm. The phnobe nodded absently and peered back across the plain. The nearest pup was trembling now, violently, and a thin plume of vapour was coming from three swollen glands around its broad rump.

'The robot was bitten by a dog,' murmured Hrsh-Hgn. 'It'ss been ssomewhat exciting up here. *Cave canem!'*

They hit the grass. An explosion dug a crater in front of them. A hot wind whipped over the sweetgrass, driving a boiling cloud of greasy black smoke. In an instant a false night fell.

Above it the sunpup wobbled into the air on three blinding blue flames. Slowly, following the route its ancestors had taken a million years before to escape a hostile world, it rose above the plains.

It gained speed and height, blew a smoke ring, and was still accelerating when Dom lost it in the distant cirrus.

Calculations:

Hrsh-Hgn manipulated a small slideball.

'I'm relieved to ssay it could not work,' he said.

'There are two suits in the *One Jump*,' said Dom. 'One ought to fit you.'

Two miles away a sunpuppy rose baying on a spreading cone of smoke.

'Look at it this way,' began Isaac persuasively.

'If we attack Madam with whirling memory swords she'll stop playing and start blasting. I dare say she won't see Dom hurt but . . . what do you rate your chances?'

'Better a boiled lamb than a roasst sheep.'

'There's no fuel in the *One Jump*,' said Dom.

'Not a drop,' added Isaac.

'It's the only way.'

Another puppy thundered upwards on a vast ventral explosion of gas. Hrsh-Hgn watched it go, his big rheumy eyes betraying a storm of mixed emotions.

'But I am no good with animalsss!' he wailed.

It was defeat. Dom and Isaac looked at each other and nodded.

Fifteen minutes later the *Drunk* sank into the grass by the empty yacht. Joan surveyed her bodyguard impatiently.

'Twenty of you and they got away!'

'The Class Five robot precipitated an illogical series of events,' explained Twelve.

'He was a Class Five mind. He told us to count to three,' added Nineteen helpfully.

'Then he hit us,' said Twelve.

'When we get back to civilization I'll see to it that the robot is lobotomized,' said Joan grimly. 'Why did we ever start building human robots?'

'The Class Fives were constructed because of

their . . .' began Twelve, and was intelligent enough to stop when Joan looked at him.

Four more robots trudged in, carrying the prone bodies of Three and Eight.

'I feel sad,' said Twelve.

'May they rust in peace,' echoed Nineteen.

'When they're recalibrated I'll make sure they go down a class,' muttered Joan. 'Right. The rest of you spread out. We won't leave till they're found.'

Ten miles eastward three sunpuppies blasted upwards. They wobbled a little, trying to stabilize the extra weight, then soared towards the stars.

Hrsh-Hgn wailed that he appeared to be in a fast-decaying orbit, but you couldn't hurry negotiations with a sundog.

She hung above them, and her name was Gully-Triode-stroke-Pledge-Hudsons-Bay-Preferred.

'The pups did reach orbit safely,' said Dom patiently.

Nevertheless, it was a despicable act, Man. The safety of our young is of paramount importance to us.

Dom thought very quickly.

'I carry the seed of Chatogaster,' he intoned.

Any friend of the lake is a friend of mine, Buster. Possibly a large payment into the sundog account would make amends for the crime which happened to be witnessed by Us alone. What is your name?

'Dom Sabalos.'

The name has a familiar ring. We have heard it recently. However. The Chain Stars are on the rim of the bubble. It will be a long time in interspace.

'The robot can take it. My friend and I have our suits. My friend is nearing re-entry,' said Dom, adopting the sundog's clipped style.

It was a long, long time in interspace.

Dom told himself that he knew that they were safe inside the sundog's field, but that didn't stop him from holding on to the beast's hide until his hands ached. The suit provided a strong depressive that made the naked images merely unpleasant. Hrsh-Hgn had passed out. Isaac had shut down most of his circuits.

It was a *long* time.

9

'They should not exist. They are theoretically possible, but so is balancing a needle on the end of a hair. Faced with something like the Chain Stars a man must either bow the knee, or else get good and worried.'

Charles Sub-Lunar, *Galactic Excursions*

Dom wondered what was so impressive. That was when the Chain was still twenty AUs away, and side on.

Then the Creapii shuttle came in closer.

Imagine a doughnut, three million miles across. Imagine another. Link them.

The Chain Stars. And tumbling around them, Minos – a planet formed from thousands of asteroids, dragged across the light years and fused into a world. That was another Joker achievement, the Maze on Minos.

The cabin was empty except for shape-adaptable seats and the screen. From outside it had appeared gigantic, several times bigger than an average cargo ship and surprisingly stream-lined. Dom knew that most of the bulk must be shielding, plus an engine big enough to lift the ship up against the crushing pull of a sun. But the streamlining puzzled him.

Until he realized. Even suns have atmospheres.

The glowing, linked rings grew rapidly in the screen, until the outer edges slipped away. It was no comfort to know the image was just that, an image darkened and screened down until it was merely bright. Instinct said they were plunging into the heart of a star.

'Born of the sun, we travel a little way towards the sun,' misquoted Isaac, tactlessly. Dom relaxed, and laughed. He thought he could hear a muted thunder, not unlike the roar of star flames. It was impossible, of course. It was just that he thought he could hear it. Of course, it was impossible.

Finally all definition was lost, and the screen became a painfully white rectangle. Hrsh-Hgn was trembling with a phnobe's instinctive fear of naked sunlight. Dom pictured the ship coasting over a glowing sea, one with no horizon, and stopped his imagination resolutely when he thought of all the little mechanical things that could go wrong.

Something was drastically wrong with the raft when it appeared.

Artists and the eye of imagination portrayed a raft only a few steps removed from the log platforms that dagon fishers used, with perhaps a few Creapii slithering nonchalantly across the deck, and it was open to the sky, with a class of a yellow ocean a long way beneath. But even High-Degrees could not survive in the open except on near-cinders stars, and the Chains Raft was one of the first on a hot star. It was just a blank hemisphere, hovering flat side down in what appeared on the screen as a thin mist.

The shuttle docked gently, and a section of wall slid back to reveal a circular grey tunnel. A friendly mechanical voice invited them to follow it. Dom led the way, warily.

The sound he heard hit him like a club. He ran forward, unbelieving.

It was the sea.

His Furness CReegE + 690° rolled down to the beach on bright caterpillar tracks. He was big, much bigger than the low-degree Creapii that lived on Widdershins. His egg-shaped suit was golden. A fawn pranced by his side, and a small blue singing bird was perched on his tentacle. His Furness stopped at the surf line and waited patiently.

Dom felt his toes touch the sand and waded through the waves. Some of the strangeness of the Creap was gone now. He knew that he was looking at a creature who was the leader of the most advanced subspecies of a race ten times as old as men. Was the featureless ovoid looking at him? What did it see?

An armoured tentacle handed him a towel. It was rough and smelled of lemons.

'A pleasant swim?' The light tenor voice materialized without visible means of support.

'Thank you, yes,' said Dom. He opened his hand, and showed the Creap a small purple shell.

'*Trivia monarcha sinistrale*,' said the Creap. 'The Widdershine ink cowrie. Beautiful in its simplicity. How did you find my ocean?'

Dom looked back at the waves. The surf was faked. The horizon was a masterpiece of illusion, and was a hundred metres from the shore. An artificial sun set in a splendour that was real. An evening star hung in the crimson glow.

'Convincing,' he said.

The Creap laughed pleasantly, and led him slowly up the beach.

There was more land than sea in the sanctuary. Again, the Creapii had only erred on the side of generosity. On one side a plain of golden grass rippled all the way to distant mountains, crystal clear. Gods might live on those towering peaks. On the other side the forest began. A respectable stream gushed from an outcrop and meandered between root-buttressed banks; a dragonfly, one of the large Terra Novaean *aeschans*, skimmed over the water. Short turf grew between the trees, studded with gentians. Rabbits had left signs of their passing. There was a stand of fragrant fennel, and a vine twisted itself among the nearest trees. In the far distance was a volcano.

'Shall I speak to you of back projection, hidden devices, artificial irrigation?' asked His Furness innocently. Dom sniffed the air. It smelled of rain.

'I won't quite believe you,' he said. 'If I dug in the soil here, what would I find?'

'Topsoil, a fossil or two, carefully selected.'

'And?'

'Oh, rock. Limestone to a depth of three metres.'

'And then?'

'Alas for illusion: in this order, the machine level, a metre of monomolecular copper, a mere film of oxidized iron, a suspicion of a matrix field. Shall I go deeper?'

'That's deep enough, Your Furness.'

'Shall we continue our walk, then? I must feed the carp.'

Later, when the golden fish had flocked to the ringing of a little brass bell, he said: 'Must there be a reason? Then let it be that I study humanity. Earth humanity in particular. Although in saying that, I am aware of a misapprehension. Let it be said, instead, that in applying myself to the study of Totality I endeavour to do so from the human viewpoint, do you understand? It is a truism that the environment moulds the mind, and so . . .' He waved a tentacle to include the sea, the forest, the distant mountains. 'Of course, it would be easier to move onto a human world, but not so convenient.'

Dom reminded himself, forcibly, that beneath his feet burned a natural furnace. But the Creapii also studied the Chain Stars, from real close up, and His Furness had hinted that there were a number of other experiments taking place on the raft.

'The Jokers?' said the Creap. 'Certainly I will help if I can. You are our first non-Creap visitors. Do you know of any prophecies in your culture concerning a green man with the sea in a bottle?'

'No,' said Dom, suddenly alarmed. 'Are there any?'

'Not that I know of. It sounds the very meat and drink of prophecy, however.

'You must realize that we are in no position to offer much advice, we need several tens of thousands of years of study. Have you any specific questions?'

'The Creapii were not the Jokers.'

'True. But that was a statement.'

'Very well. You are the oldest race, as a race. You can't count Chatogaster or the Bank, they're individual organisms. So it should follow that you are the most like the Jokers. Mentally, I mean. No, not even that. I mean in outlook.'

The Creap laughed. 'And what is our outlook?'

'You study other lifeforms. Man the Hunter, Creap the Information-Gatherer. May I be personal?'

'Please do,' said the great golden egg, and Dom blushed.

'Well, I've met Creapii before. Do you know what has always struck me as odd about them? And about you, Your Furness. You're so human.

'Hrsh-Hgn is my friend, but he is a phnobe. He gives himself away all the time, and he's lived on Widdershins, among Earth-stock humanity, for most of his life. Little things – ways of looking at life, like when we both look at the same thing and I know he's seeing it from an entirely different racial viewpoint. But all the Creapii I have met don't give that impression.'

'We live on hot worlds. We are sexless, octopoid. Human?' said CReegE + 690°.

'Chel! Humanity is a state of mind, not body. But that is a point. I wondered, why do they seem so like me, when they must be so alien? I think it's because all the Creapii I've met have consciously tried to adopt the human viewpoint. They're Humans first, Creapii second.'

Dom faced the egg, except that it had no face. At length the disembodied voice said: 'There is a great deal in what you say.'

'I think you do this to gain a greater understanding of the universe,' said Dom. 'Men see a different universe to phnobes. I'm sorry, I keep picking the wrong words. They *experience* a different universe. Is that right?'

'That is very sapient. Before we dine with the others, would you like to see something?'

They found him an eggsuit, fitted out for visitors with a simple control panel. It was like riding in a small, vertical tank. In Dom's case it was to keep the heat out, rather than in. Then he ventured into the main section of the raft.

He couldn't remember very much afterwards. Individual experiences blended into a montage of heat, large, slithering galaxy-shaped monsters, the thunder of the sun and a strange flickering in the air. He did remember being led to an observation platform, set in the middle of a matrix-coil, and being invited to look up.

The circular star on which the raft was moored was just passing under the arch of its twin. On a cooler world the experience would have been enough to inspire a dozen religions.

A shining arch, only marginally brighter than the sky around it, moved across the solar sky.

He didn't know if the other Creapii were aware that the clumsily driven suit held a young man rather than a drunken Creap, if Creapii drank. Probably they didn't. After an hour of it he felt drunk.

It lasted for several minutes after he was back in the sanctuary. CReegE did not have to point out the lesson. By something like osmosis he had been given just a feeling of Creapiness. The

Creap had been trying to tell him that he was right. The world of the Creapii was a Totality away from the world of men. So the Creaps tried to think – to feel – like men. Only thus could the whole nature of the universe be comprehended, they said.

With a new understanding Dom realized that the official view of the Creapii was wrong. They were said to be the race born to science. Creapii were the cool-heads of the universe, the ultimate analysers, a race of intelligent robots, had robots been what the first robotic pioneers considered them to be. It just wasn't true. What was it one of the pre-Sadhim sects had striven for? Ultimate reality? That was it. The Creapii were the mystics of the universe.

They ate at a table under a spreading pear tree. A stew of slightly rotting oily black toadstools, a real delicacy, had been provided for Hrsh-Hgn. Isaac ate Whole Erse potatoes for energy. There was a seafood soufflé for Dom, expertly cooked. He was beginning to realize too that Creapii were experts automatically. His Furness sucked something from a pressurized cylinder into an airlock approximately where his stomach should have been.

'Where is your next port of call?' he asked.

'Minos, if you can take me there,' said Dom. 'I have to get another ship, and I know there is a multiracial settlement there. I could take a look at the Maze, too.'

'Do you think there might be a clue in the Maze?' asked the Creap politely.

Isaac chortled, and nudged Dom heavily in the ribs.

'That was a clever literary allusion, that was,' he said. 'Even the name of the planet is—'

'I know,' said Dom. 'I shall look forward to meeting the minotaur. Hrsh?'

'Oh, nothing,' said the phnobe, looking up. 'I was jusst reflecting that I sseem to be insside a legend.'

He called the ship *One Jump Behind*. It was the best the small yard on Minos had to offer. It lacked even an autochef, which was a point in its favour, but its matrix was carefully calibrated and the cabin was at least larger than a closet.

'Why *One Jump Behind*?' asked Isaac.

'Relativity,' said Dom. 'It's full name ought to be *A Jump So Far Ahead That If Einstein Had Been Right It Would End Right Behind You*. Try getting that on the ident panel. Do you think you can handle it?'

'It'll do,' said Isaac ruefully. 'It's hardly a thoroughbred.'

They walked through the human scientific colony towards the Maze, the nearest wall of which loomed over the low domes.

'What did you think of the High-Degrees?' said Hrsh-Hgn.

183

'Remarkable,' said Dom non-committally. 'What about you?'

'I met several while you were taken on that tour. I wass sstruck by their phnobisshness, ass you might expect, and your ssuggesstion that each race ssees itss reflection in the—'

A small silver egg rolled up to them at the Maze entrance, waving a sheaf of papers in a tentacle. The reddish tint of its eyeshield said it was a very low-degree Creap indeed.

'Psst!' hissed a non-directional voice. 'Wanna buy a map? Can't see the Maze without a map. Compiled by my brood-brother from genuine aerial photographs!'

'Sod off, cinderbrain!' screamed a large Creap, thundering towards the group. 'Now, sir and frss, you are obviously discerning people and you want a map. Now I have a map, sir and frss, the like of which is seldom seen.'

'Do I need a map?' Dom asked.

'Not precissely,' said the phnobe, who had visited the Maze before. 'But they do make good souvenirss!'

A dozen other map-sellers lurched and rolled after them as they strode into the Maze.

The Jokers had their little joke. Occasionally a researcher would point out that the Maze was probably never designed as a maze at all, but none could come up with a believable alternative use. Dom wasn't surprised when his two companions faded away on either side of him –

Hrsh-Hgn had warned him of the Maze effect.

Something in the monomolecular walls created a separate universe for every individual. That was why all maps and aerial photographs ceased to be useful. Dom's own map of the maze could be perfectly accurate – for Dom.

Once he saw a shadowy outline of Hrsh-Hgn walk out of a wall and disappear into another. Dom thumped the wall good and hard and then, glancing around to make sure that no one was watching, played a stripper beam over the white surface. It didn't even get hot. As an illusion it was pretty solid.

He found the centre after ten minutes' brisk walking. He had the memory sword still turned to the stripper setting, and his finger hovered on the stud as Ways turned round and smiled.

'I see you were expecting me,' he said pleasantly.

Dom fired. Ways gave him a hurt look, and extended a hand. A growing, light-bending sphere bounced towards Dom and disappeared.

'Round One,' said Ways. 'Now *I've* a resonance-dampening matrix, but what have you got?'

'Who are you?' said Dom. He thumbed the weapon on its knife setting.

'Ways of Earth.' He stopped and tossed the knife back to Dom. 'I'm afraid you have blunted the blade,' he continued, 'but that was a pretty smart throw.'

'My next question was have you come to kill me, but that's not intelligent, is it?'

'No,' said Ways, 'I don't seem to be achieving anything, but I must keep trying otherwise what is free will for?'

'Do I get any explanations?'

'Sure. You must realize that the universe is too big to hold us and the Jokers. Some people are afraid that the Jokers might turn up any day now.'

'Do they expect some kind of big-brained monsters?'

'I think gods are what they are expecting. You know where you are with big-brained monsters, but gods are another matter. No one wants to be a slave race. Oh, I've got a couple of things for you.'

The robot slid aside his chest panel and threw Ig at Dom. The little animal screamed vengeance at Ways from the safety of its master's shoulder, then dived inside Dom's shirt.

'And there was something else . . .' said the robot. He patted his carry-all, and felt around behind his chestplate. 'Sorry for the delay, you know how it is, thing wanted never there. Ah, here.'

Dom caught the small grey sphere before he could stop himself. It was warm. Ways watched him closely.

'That is a matrix engine without a coil,' he said. 'By now it should have blown your head off. Crude, I know.'

186

Dom hurled the globe over the nearest wall. It sparkled briefly under the light of the Chains before landing with a thud in the next avenue. Then Ways cannoned into him.

The robot had weight behind him. Dom rolled backwards and tried to throw his attacker, and had to jerk aside as a fist struck the Maze floor by his ear. The blow split the artificial skin. Ways turned the punch into a sideswipe, and a fingertip scored a cut across the boy's head.

Ig erupted straight for the eyes. Ways brushed him off lightly, and leapt back, flexing his fingers.

'I refuse to believe in invulnerability,' he said. 'Let's get down to the real thing.'

The matrix engine exploded. The Maze thumped.

Ways was picked up like a doll and hurled at the wall, one flailing leg catching Dom across the chest.

And a long way overhead a ship was coming in to land.

10

'On Laoth they cultivate with a screwdriver.'
Galactic Miscellany

'Hark to the crash of
the leaves in the autumn, the smash
of the crystal leaves.'
Charles Sub-Lunar, *Planetary Haiku*

The bed was a relic, an ornate black affair that
bore all the markings of the Taminic-P'ing
Dynasty. Dom stared through thinning blue
mists at the rest of the room.

He was in a treasure house. Or it may have
been a museum. Someone had ferried furniture
and ornaments across the galaxy and dumped
them there with no regard for style and period.
Memory tapestries hung from two of the walls,
where forgotten heroes re-enacted pages from
history like an ever-repeating recording. A set of
tstame men in ceremonial costume stood stiffly

to attention on a board set in a giant cultured ruby. There was a water sculpture, inactive, which lay in a pool at the bottom of its tank, and an Early Chrome display case displaying several pieces of bootlegged Phnobic temple pottery. Where the walls were free of tapestries they were hung with purple drapes.

Dom pictured the severely practical home domes on Widdershins. The only ornamentation really encouraged was the Sadhim logo and perhaps the One Commandment, suitably framed. Even electricity was allowed to come no further than the kitchen. And the Sabalos family was rich – so rich, in fact, that it could afford the simple life. Whoever owned this room was either poorer or would make them look like paupers.

He felt something warm by his ear, and turned to find Ig curled up in the sleeping field. The creature opened one eye and purred.

Dom swung himself clumsily out of the bed's field and landed clumsily. The gravity was fractionally higher than Widdershins.

He drew aside a curtain and saw a sun, flattened by refraction, dipping below a rugged horizon. It was an anaemic red. And something small flew jerkily past the window, found an open section and flittered in. Dom saw the metallic sheen of its wings as it hovered around the light, and the haze of its tiny airscrew. It was a Laoth moth. The sun out there was Tau Ceti, and it was setting pale because the atmosphere was almost dust-free. He felt pleased with himself.

The bronze doors at the far end of the room swung open, and Isaac walked in.

'Hi, boss,' he said wearily. 'How do you feel?'

'My chest feels like someone's been sticking pokers in it,' said Dom, ruefully. 'The last I remember I was on Minos.'

'That's right. We found you at the entrance to the Maze with your chest half caved in. That Ig was keening fit to bust.'

Dom sat down. 'At the entrance to the Maze? How did I get there? Hey – did you look in the centre?'

The robot nodded. 'Sure, but our centres, if you see what I mean. Another attempt, huh?' Dom told him.

Isaac said: 'Your grandmother arrived not long after. Hrsh-Hgn and I thought well, you were dying, and the *Drunk* is a fast ship.'

'Yes, okay. But this isn't Widdershins.'

'She stopped off here so you could get treatment. Those googoo bodies aren't infinitely self-repairing.'

'Of course, this is your home, isn't it?'

Isaac stiffened. 'I am a citizen of the galaxy, boss. Yes, this is the old place. Workship Three, Factory Complex Nineteen, that's where I sprang from.' He looked round the room. 'Mind you, we never got to see the inside of this place. Between

190

ourselves, I don't like it. Do you know I'm the only 'bot in the place?'

'Knock it off, there must be servants!' said Dom, looking for some clothes.

'Sure. Humans. I tell no lie, sahib.'

Dom gaped at him.

'And one of them called me "sir"! In my cube, any human who calls a robot "sir" is due for a bunch of knuckles.'

'Cool down and find me some clothes. I want to see this place before it vanishes,' said Dom.

They walked out of the room and along a broad, deep-carpeted corridor. Isaac led the way through several large, over-furnished halls until they reached a pair of silvered doors. Two men in brown and gold livery opened the doors hurriedly and stood to attention as they passed through; Dom heard a mechanical growl in Isaac's throat.

A circular table with a central well filled the room. Dom's gaze first caught Joan; she dominated the room, as usual, in a long midnight-purple dress and a black wig that matched her skin. She smiled faintly. Next to her was a tall, fat man, built almost on drosk lines; Dom recognized him as the Emperor Ptarmigan. Next to him was Keja, even at this moment rising from her seat before racing round the table to embrace Dom. By her sat a boy about Dom's age, regarding him thoughtfully.

The rest of the table was made up of the usual run of Board directors and senior planetary management.

Keja embraced Dom and kissed him.

'I knew you'd turn up here! Dom, you're green . . .' she gasped. 'Have you been fishing?'

'Sort of,' he said.

'Come and join us, we were just starting dinner. Tarli, could you move along? If you crush up a bit Isaac can find room, too,' she added brightly.

'Sure,' said the boy, grinning at Dom.

'Me, madam? Dine with humans?' said Isaac coldly, gazing fixedly at the liveried men standing behind the diners.

'Don't be embarrassed – we're all one big integrated circuit here,' said Keja.

Dom leaned close to the robot and murmured: 'Sit down and look pleasant or I will personally disassemble you with nails, teeth and toes.'

Dom ended up sitting between the Emperor, who greeted him politely before turning back to Joan, and Keja. Many of the diners were watching Dom with frank disbelief. There were several phnobes around the table, with Hrsh-Hgn hissing amicably to a very important-looking alpha-male.

'Do you always dine like this?' he asked.

'Oh, yes,' said Keja, 'Ptarmigan prefers to have people where he can see them.' She raised a finger and the waiters moved forward.

'Uh, Keja, how long have I been here?'

'Since yesterday night. You're famous, little brother. According to Ptarmigan half the galaxy is out looking for you. You're supposed to be leading us all to Jokers World. What do you think we'll find there?'

'On present showing, a damn great bomb.' He saw her flinch. 'Sorry, I didn't mean that. Famous, eh?'

'There's a dozen ships in orbit, most of them Terra Novaean and Whole Erse. More turn up every hour. Ptarmigan is very angry about it. I haven't quite understood it all, but I gather that everyone wants to kidnap you. Is it true that you'll discover Jokers World in five days' time, whatever happens?'

'I expect so. How come everyone knows?'

'Well, you haven't been keeping it a secret, have you? United Spies are in on it too. Ptarmigan has to send special squads out every hour to sweep up those little robot insects they keep dropping on the palace. One got into the kitchen and opened the oven on a soufflé, and that's outside all the rules!'

'Is one of the ships Creapii?'

'I don't know.'

Tarli leaned round his young stepmother and nodded. 'My apologies, O Dom, but I have been overhearing the conversation—'

'Eavesdropping,' said Keja sternly.

'—and as a matter of fact one of the ships is

a Crepii VMFTL squareship, Chain Stars registration.'

'Chain Stars, eh? Oh, boy.' A thought struck
him and his hand flew to his belt. 'Keja, was
there a bottle—'

'It's safe. My maid said one of the security men
told her that it contains the Water of Life. Not
that I'm prying, of course.'

'Of course not. In the last few days I've nearly
been killed, overdrawn at the Bank, I've
breathed for an hour underwater, I've got into
orbit by a very bawdy method, and I've had a
swim on the surface of a star. Oh yes. And I
walked out of the Maze on Minos even though
my chest was smashed up. Life is one gay round.
Someone ought to start writing my biography
now, before it's too late!'

'Try him, then,' said Keja, indicating a diner
on the far side of the table. Dom recognized the
scarred man and his battered robot.

'That's Charles Sub-Lunar, isn't it? The one
they call the Renaissance Man?'

Keja saw the man and the robot looking at
them, and raised her glass and smiled. Under
cover of this she said: 'Yes, and Joker expert.
And historian. His poetry is rather good, too. Did
you know he was the one who deciphered the
Joker language?'

'The poet and the mad computer,' quoted
Dom.

'Yes, though he's not really mad. I don't know

who the poet was. His servant is quite fascinating, too, don't you think he looks fascinating with all those scars, Dom? Dom?'

'Uh, yes,' said Dom, slowly. He twirled his wineglass thoughtfully. 'Funny, isn't it, you form an impression of people . . . I think I'd like a word with him. Excuse me.'

Dom sidled round the table, but had not been careful enough. Joan caught him lightly by the arm – lightly it looked, at least, but there was a knowledge of anatomy behind the hold.

'Good evening, Grandson. You have been mixing with some very bad company, it seems. Ways is the chief torpedo of the Joker Institute.'

Dom sighed. 'All right, Grandmother. I suppose you have been prying into my mind?'

'Well, you were unconscious and it naturally seemed the logical thing to do.'

'Oh, naturally.'

'Don't be peevish, this is real life. Every security man in the galaxy knows about Ways. Once he assassinated the deputy-chief of United Spies, you know. He's a robot with a killer instinct. I see you've still got that swamp crawler?'

'He's spent a little time with Ways. I think it's likely that he's been booby-trapped,' said Dom. 'I wouldn't worry too much.'

'You think you're invulnerable. Don't bank on it,' said Joan. She glared at Ig.

The Emperor rose slowly to his feet and rang a small black bell. The diners began to leave the

195

table. Dom saw Sub-Lunar and his serving man disappear into the crowd.

'What happens now?' he asked. 'I understand everyone's waiting for me to make a move.'

'Are you going to discover Jokers World?'

Most of the diners had left. The Emperor bowed to them and left them seated. Across the room Hrsh-Hgn and Isaac chatted to Tarli.

'I think so,' said Dom. 'I'm getting the . . . the sort of outline of it already. It's not a planet. I mean, it may be a planet but . . . well, Widdershins is a planet, with an orbit, a hydrosphere and a magnetic field and so on, but Widdershins is also a world and a culture.'

'I see,' said Joan. 'I wonder where it could be?'

'I've got five days, less now, so that rules out most places outside the life-bubble. I think . . .' Dom stopped. 'You are pumping me.'

'For the sake of Widdershins. I don't want you to find Jokers World and lose it to a mob. You don't care about politics. I tell you, used properly this could be the making of the Sabalos family.'

'You mean that seriously?'

'I do.' She rose. 'We'll talk about this later. Are you coming to see the Masque?'

'You must!' said Tarli, hurrying round the table. 'It's a special production. Sub-Lunar wrote it on the ship coming here. Father likes a little entertainment after dinner.'

*   *   *

Dom thought it was mildly entertaining. It was a skit on current Earth-Outer Worlds politics, which were always good for a laugh, written in early Greek style. All the characters wore larger-than-life masks, spangled with jewels. The chorus was robotic.

Then it nailed Dom to his seat.

The chief protagonist was a goat-legged Chairman Pan, complete with horn and syrynx. It happened after the bit of business with the First Sirian Bank, a bloated silver globe on spindly legs.

The Bank said: 'DO YOU THINK, THEN, THAT MAN CAN PREVENT HIMSELF BEING OUSTED BY ROBOTS?'

Pan capered across the stage: 'Certainly. What robot could do my job? They can only go down to Class Ones, you know.'

Chorus: 'Brekekekex, co-ax, co-axial!'

Pan: 'But list! Who is this weary traveller?'

Another actor lurched onto the stage. He was a bright, vivid green. He was staggering under the combined weight of a pair of winged sandals that left a trail of feathers, a large sword made of rubber, a giant bottle of water and, on one emerald shoulder, a taxidermist's nightmare of glass eyeballs, feathers, tufts of hair and badly assorted claws.

Pan: 'Good grief! What are you doing with that strange, ill-assorted creature?'

Traveller: 'It's not a strange creature, it's my pet.'

Pan: 'I was talking to your pet. What do you seek, traveller? Get on with it so we can continue with this sketch.'

The traveller peered myopically around the stage and then glared at the audience.

'I'm looking for a world of Jokers,' he muttered.

Pan said: 'Try Earth. They are quite good-humoured on Terra Novae, too. Oh, *those* Jokers. Be off with you! They don't exist – do they?'

'Yes and no. That is, no and yes.'

Bank: 'EVERYONE KNOWS THEY HAVE MOVED TO THE UNIVERSE NEXT DOOR—'

Pan: '—so why not look on the dark side of the sun?'

Traveller. 'Gosh, yes! The dark side of the sun, you say? I'll go there directly.' He shuffled off.

Dom woke next morning in a bedroom almost oppressive in its wealth, washed in a gold bowl and strolled down to the dining hall. He was late for breakfast. Most of the night had been spent in a fruitless discussion with Joan. There had been a row when Ig was taken to a laboratory and probed for every conceivable weapon, to the little animal's distress. Nothing was found, but Ig, coiled across Dom's shoulders, was strangely silent today.

Sub-Lunar had left after the Masque, after taking an urgent call from Earth.

Down in the hall a floating sideboard had been laid out with large dishes under covers. Dom padded silently over the carpet, experimentally lifting lids. One covered a dish of smoked red fish, another the considerable wreckage of a boar's head. A third was just fruit. Being a Widdershine, he settled at last for the fish, and sat down at one end of the empty table. Out of interest he lifted the lid of a large tureen, and slammed it down hurriedly; the Emperor had been entertaining drosk guests.

A few minutes later a small door across the hall opened and a girl tiptoed in. She was small, and dark like Tarli. Dom grinned. She blushed, and sidled along the sideboard with her eyes fixed on him.

She piled a small dish with little fish and sat down at the opposite side of the table. Dom stared at her. In the morning light she seemed to glow. It was uncanny. The glow followed her, so that when she moved an arm she left a faint, golden ghost in the air. An electro-physical effect, but still impressive.

They ate in silence, broken only by the hum of a large, antique Standard clock.

Finally he steeled himself. 'Can you speak Janglic? Linaka Comerks diwac? How about drosk? – upaquaduc, uh, lapidiquac nunquackuqc quipaduckuadicquakak?'

She poured herself a tiny cup of coffee and smiled at him. Dom groaned inwardly. Drosk was bad enough, but he could handle it. He prepared his epiglottis and sinuses for the supreme test.

'Ffnbasshs sFFshs – frs Sfghn Gss?'

Her second smile struck him as unnecessarily prim. She clapped her hands. A moment later he felt a presence by his elbow.

A giant was standing behind his chair. A pair of eye-slits surveyed him dispassionately from a small head atop a body as broad as it was high, which was almost two metres. It wore a jerkin of leather, covered with familiar angular designs in red and blue. A variety of hand weapons were stuck into the belt. It was a drosk – an old one – so of course it was a female. If there had been any males in the place they were probably in her deep-freeze right now.

The girl sang a glissando of bell-like note. The red eyes blinked.

'Empress say what you say?'

'I was just trying to be sociable,' said Dom. 'Who are you?'

The giant held a brief interchange with the girl, and said, 'I her bodyguard and lady-of-the-bedchamber.'

'That must be economical.'

'Lady Sharli say you come for a ride?'

Without waiting for his answer the drosk lifted him out of his chair with one hand. Ig woke up and bared his teeth, then whined as the giant picked him up gently in another great paw and crooned to him. The swamp ig blinked, then ran up one iron-muscled arm and perched on the drosk's head.

Sharli was already walking across the broad patio outside the hall. She looked sympathetically at Dom as he was dumped at her feet like a parcel, and stamped her foot – to Dom's amazement, for even his mother had never resorted to that in her expert tantrums – and waved one tiny finger at the giant, who bowed to her. She helped Dom to his feet.

A robot was standing holding the reins of two creatures. Dom hadn't seen horses before, except the pair that had been regretfully sent back on his birthday. But these were Laothian horses. Therefore they were robots.

Sharli was helped onto one with a coat of anodized aluminium. The reins were some woven metal, hung with jewels and bells.

Dom's mount was copper coloured. As he climbed into the control saddle it turned and looked at him through multifaceted eyes, and said: 'Can you ride, buster?'

'I don't know, I've never tried.'

'Okay, then let me to the work, huh?' said the horse, pawing the ground.

'What did they put a Class Five brain in a horse for?' Dom asked as they walked away from the palace, with the drosk trotting behind.

'I'm kept for guests. You gotta be intelligent

with some of them,' said the horse conversationally. 'You the guy who's going to discover this great El-Ay in the sky?'

'Yes. Have you ever met a Class Five, registration TR-3B4-5?' asked Dom.

'Oh, him. We were programmed together. He went off to serve some backplanet king, and I got landed with this.'

'I thought you might have known my Isaac. You've got the same conversational style,' he said.

'Being a horse isn't too bad,' said the horse, tossing its head. 'They gotta treat me well, on account of us Class Fives being officially Human. You get regular overhauls and three jolts a day . . . Did you say something?'

'I'm thinking,' said Dom. He bit his lip and stared at the scenery.

Nothing grew on Laoth. The planet was sterile. Incoming ships went through a rigorous decontamination and visitors were stripped of everything except necessary colonic bacteria. Laoth's atmosphere had been imported. A world with an economy based on the manufacture of electronic miracles couldn't afford one tiny virus in the wrong place.

But a bare world was inhuman. So, around his palace, another Emperor Ptarmigan, the first of the dynasty, started to build a garden . . .

Rooted in barren dust, powered by sunlight, the robot acres were deader than a corpse but, like a corpse, roared with tiny life.

Electronic men were a fact of life. A fifth of the Human population was metal. Electronic nature was something else again.

The stately copper trees were nevertheless squat and gnarled like oaks to support their selenium-cell leaves, which tinkled in the breeze. Hummingbirds – an electronic hum – whirred among the spun-silver flowers, where small golden bees tapped the currents into their tiny batteries and flew back to their secret, dark storage cells. In a little mineral-rich brook that wound through the garden the reeds sucked up the metals and threw forth brittle sulphur flowers. In the depths, zinc trout churned. And in the cool pools aluminium water lilies opened like hands.

The horses trotted between the trees and along gravel paths lined with nodding flowers. Sharli led him to a small hill where a steamlet gushed out of the ground and fell over a rock outcrop into a deep blue pool. A small pagoda had been built amid beds of golden lilies, shot with copper.

She sat down and patted the seat beside her, then spoke to the giant.

'Lady Sharli say to tell about yourself,' the drosk said. She was throwing a two-foot knife in the air and catching it by the blade.

He did. There were long pauses when the giant translated, and he had plenty of time to watch a little brass spider which scuttled out of a cranny a few feet above his head and, taking up a position on a steel twig, swung purposely outward.

Sharli was a good audience, and possibly the giant was a good interpreter. The girl gasped at the account of the fight in the Bank, and laughed and clapped her hands, weaving a golden haze in the air, when he told her about the escape by sunpuppy.

The spider climbed another twig and swung again.

'Empress say, were you not scared?'

Dom tried to explain the predictions while the spider completed several more jumps. He hadn't finished before the spider had completed a web of fine copper wire and retired to a twig, paying out two tiny power cables behind it.

Dom told himself that he was being too expansive, too sure of himself. But Sharli was gazing at him wide-eyed. It was too much to resist. Besides, her perfume was going to his head. He was acutely aware of the giant lady's maid behind him, and the horse, too, had sniggered once or twice.

While he was demonstrating his grav sandals by flying a figure-of-eight above her head a small mechanical fly blundered into the spider web. There was a minute blue flash.

Prowess in catching and steering windshells was being explained while the spider slowly dismantled the protesting fly with two spanner-like legs.

Another horse galloped between the trees. At the controls was Tarli, almost hidden in an armour made of leather slabs in a complex over-lapping pattern. He removed his fearsome helmet, wiped his forehead with his gauntlet, and smiled brightly at Dom.

'Greetings, step-uncle. I thought you might be here. I hope you have not been overly bored?'

'Not at all,' said Dom airily. 'Er, your cos-tume . . .'

Tarli raised his eyebrows. 'I have been sham fighting. You do not fight sham on Widder-shins?'

Dom thought of one or two fights he had seen on the jetties, when four-foot-long dagon-knives were used. 'It's usually for real on Widdershins,' he said. 'Sham?'

Tarli unslung a long bundle from his horse and drew out a sword as tall as he was. The handle was leather-bound, with no superfluous decoration. The blade was invisible, except when it caught the light, when it showed up momen-tarily as a thin green sliver.

'Shamsword,' he explained. 'The blade is, of course, only a few microns thick, forged as a molecule in the special sword-light of dawn. Strong, too. Perhaps you are a good swords-man?'

'I can use a memory sword,' said Dom. He drew his own and demonstrated. Tarli took it gingerly.

'How does it work?'

'There's a little matrix field projector in the stud that can generate up to a dozen shapes.'

Tarli handed it back. 'Not an honourable weapon,' he said sadly. 'You would perhaps like a sham battle?'

He laughed at Dom's expression and pulled two wooden lathes from his bundle. 'For practice,' he explained. 'So novices don't lose too many appendages in the learning. I am the second-best shamuri on Laoth.'

Dom felt Sharli's eye on him.

'Okay,' he said miserably. After all, he could handle a sword by proxy on the tstame board, even if it was only a two-inch skewer wielded by a mommet. And they were only wooden poles.

Tarli unpacked another helmet and some pieces of leather body armour, and Sharli helped Dom into them.

'You'd better explain the rules.'

Tarli smiled. 'This is only stick sham. Anything goes, but you've got to use the stick. Sharli will give us the signal.'

The girl, who had been watching them with interest, shook her head and spoke sharply to her brother.

'She says we've got to fight for a prize. My

206

sword against your grav sandals. I don't think that's fair.'

'Don't worry,' said Dom. He bent down and began to unstrap his sandals. Tarli sighed and laid his shamsword on the seat alongside them.

Sharli waved a small handkerchief.

The poles met in mid-air, once, and they circled each other warily.

Dom felt emboldened and tried one or two lunges, which slid harmlessly off the other's pole. Tarli smiled, and spun his pole around a finger. The spin carried on – the pole flashed across his back, was caught again and came down with a thud on the heavy padding of Dom's helmet. Tarli made a few passes and completed the movement with another gentle blow to the head.

Dom jerked aside and swung his pole downwards. Tarli hopped over it, lunged and twisted. Caught by the added leverage Dom slid several yards on his stomach in the gravel.

Sharli put her hand over her mouth and turned away. Her shoulders were shaking.

Dom's pole came down with a crack across Tarli's unprotected feet. Then he scrambled up and brought it down in a whistling arc that ended on the boy's arm.

Tarli staggered backwards, waving his arms desperately to keep his balance. Dom caught him again in the chest.

Tarli disappeared.

Dom ran forward in time to see his white face vanish under the water of the waterfall pool. He struggled out of his own armour and dived after him, hitting the water in a jangle of water lilies.

Far below him a dark shape was sinking into the depths. Dom caught it, grabbed him by the arm and kicked out for the surface. As they broke water gravity found the heavy armour again and they both went under.

He fought for the surface again, trying to find the buckles of the armour. Then a thick arm broke through the ripples and he snatched at it.

As soon as she could get a grip of Tarli's limp body the giant pushed Dom back into the water, slung the boy across her shoulder and set off at a run through the trees.

Dom hauled himself out, painfully and shame-facedly, on the rocks at the far side of the pool. He coughed up water and waited for the pounding in his head to stop.

He heard the swish of a blade, and threw himself backwards. Underwater he blundered into a thicket of finger-thick cabling, and surfaced again in a clump of water lilies. Sharli glanced at him, and let the tip of the blade take another two-foot slice out of the black rock where his fingers had been.

'He was only playing,' she hissed in perfect Janglic. 'He is the second-best shamuri in the galaxy, and he was only playing. But you had to win!'

'I am not playing,' she added. The sword sizzled round her head and took a thick copper branch off a nearby tree without noticeably slowing.

Dom dived and came up at the far side of the pool, scrambling out as she came round after him. His discarded body armour still lay in the gravel. He groped in it feverishly. It couldn't withstand a shamsword that could cut through rock. The padding was just to take the force of the blow – there must be a static field to turn that impossibly sharp edge . . .

He didn't see the blow. There was no sensation except for a faint glimmer of green. The piece of breastplate he was holding was just in two pieces, that was all. The singlet had become a doublet. It was no consolation to see sheared field components dribble out onto the ground.

'I will cut you up,' she said. 'A bit at a time. Starting with the *extremities*!'

The tip of the sword drew a thin line across his arm only because Dom had moved with commendable speed.

'You say your death won't be yet,' she said. 'Can you be so sure, hey?'

Dom winced and closed his eyes. The sword caught him in the neck. He opened his eyes, and felt her contemptuous glare as he touched his neck sheepishly.

'You wait till you nod your head. I hit you with the flat, fool!' she said, walking up to him and standing on tiptoe to bring her hand across in a stinging slap. 'Boastful, boorish, barbarian *boy!*'

His feet fought for purchase on the edge as he teetered over the pool, and then for the third time he hit the water bodily and came up shaking his head and gasping. Sharli pointed the sword at him, trembling.

'If he is dead, boy, if he is dead . . .' She picked up a small rock and threw it inexpertly at his head. When he broke surface again she was a small figure riding between the trees.

Dom let the water stream off him, and lay on the gravel watching the ants. They had appeared from everywhere to congregate around the branch that she had cut down. While he watched, it fell neatly in two, and he saw the tiny blue pinpoint of an electronic cutter. The smaller piece was dragged quickly across the gravel to a hatchway that had appeared in the tree.

Dom took his grav sandals and the shamsword and walked back to the horse. It looked at him sympathetically and said nothing. He rode off thoughtfully.

High up on the stump of the branch a minute crane was being jostled into position and scaffolding had appeared. The myrmidon reconstruction crew had already set to work.

Further up, where the silicon-chip leaves drank in the sun and tinkled in the breeze, another insect watched them impassively. It had camera eyes, and it was not a Laoth make.

A spider watched it, and thought of electricity.

11

'We are an old race. We have enjoyed all that the galaxy has to offer – I myself have seen the black mouth in the centre of the galaxy, and the bright dead stars beyond – and therefore as a race we must be doomed. You seek new experience as a pseudo-human; I study the birth of hydrogen in the interstellar abyss with the race called Pod. We sublimate our Creapiness, because it stifles us. Where do we go from here?'

Personal letter from His Furness CRabE + 687° to His Furness CReegE + 690°, reprinted in the anthology *Post Joker*

'Enter.'

Dom pushed open the door.

Tarli was lying on his stomach, reading. He glanced up and grinned. 'Come on in.'

Dom entered sheepishly and dumped the grav sandals on the bed.

'Yours,' he said. Tarli touched them thoughtfully.

'Yes,' he said, doubtfully, and switched off the cube.

'Gravity was on my side and I cheated and, well . . .' said Dom miserably.

'You're soaked,' said Tarli. He clapped his hands. There was a rush of air from one corner of the room and a young drosk appeared, took an order for clothing and a towel, and vanished. A moment later she was back.

'Have your people got, um, rigid rules about bodily exposure?' asked Tarli. 'If so, the ablution room is through there.'

Dom pulled his sodden shirt over his head and grunted.

'Only we get all sorts here, you see. Okay, Chaquaduc.' He clapped his hands again and the bowing figure disappeared. Dom glanced up.

'That's pretty neat. Field transference? Grandmother won't have it in the house. She says it's a wicked waste of power.'

Tarli held up his hand. 'Inductance surfaces under the skin, yes. It's a tradition with us. It impresses guests. Here.'

Dom caught a dragonskin belt and buckled it around a loose-fitting robe intricately worked in yellow and grey silk. The Laothian boy opened an enamelled closet and handed him a smaller version of the sword.

'Hey!'

'It's only a koto. Purely ceremonial. Please accept it. Apart from anything else, by custom it's a mortal insult if you don't. I'd have to fight you again, with swords and without armour. And before that I'd have to teach you to use it.' He glanced sidelong at Dom's neck. 'You've been getting a few lessons anyway, I hear.'

Dom's hand flew to his neck and he winced, not just from the bruises.

'I thought Laothian girls went in more for flower arranging,' he muttered.

Tarli grinned. 'Oh yes? The nearest flowers to us are on Boon-dock, the next planet out. The biggest ones are motile roses – you have to get the plant in an armlock before you can prune it.'

'I bet she'd be good at it.'

'Pretty good, probably. She's first on the shamsword lists, that's out of about five hundred true shamuri. You have to be expert to get on the lists.'

Dom fingered the blade of the koto and grunted.

'Archery, now, I'm better at that. She hasn't got the patience. Sharli's only about thirtieth in the list.'

'Anything she's not good at?'

'There's our third national pastime.'

'What's that? Pig-sticking? Crushing rocks with the fingers?'

'No. Micro-circuitry design. It's an art, you know. Come on, it's time for dinner.'

Dom was surprised as they made their way towards the main hall. He was on Laoth, a world that made the best shipware and Class Five minds that were classed as humans, and he had seen no robots apart from the horse and the mechanisms in the garden. Laothians obviously didn't like to surround themselves with their creations.

As they walked through a hall lined with lacquered panels, Tarli said slowly: 'Father is very annoyed.'

'About me?'

'Indirectly, yes. It wasn't your coming here – he likes visitors. It's just that we are getting some uninvited ones. How many days before you discover Jokers World?'

'After tonight, three days.'

'Have you got any ideas?'

'Some,' said Dom non-committally.

'I hope so,' said Tarli. 'There's fifty ships hanging around our system now, waiting for you to make a move. Some of them are toting weaponry, too. Terra Novae has got a whole fleet. There's even a class of a hulk from Whole Erse, it's probably the only one they have got. There's going to be a real shoot-out when you lead them to Jokers World. And, uh, what's worrying Father . . .'

'You can put his mind at rest. I don't think the Jokers had anything to do with Laoth,' said Dom quickly.

Tarli sighed with relief. 'The trouble they're putting us to!' he went on. 'We have to send out squads every hour to clear up these bugs United Spies are dropping round the palace. They crawl into every crevice – look at that one!'

A thing like a jewelled praying mantis was creeping along the top of one of the coloured panels. It tried to scurry away as they approached, but Tarli flicked it onto the floor with the end of his sword and crushed it.

'Looks like a standard Earth model,' he said. 'See what I mean?'

'The message behind all this is that you're glad to see me but you'd be even happier to see me go,' said Dom.

Tarli said hurriedly: 'Please don't take it the wrong way. I'll tell you one thing, we'll make sure you go vertically, and protected. Still, you're not our only worry. Have you heard about the Bank disappearing?'

Dom shook his head.

'Nothing like it has happened before.'

The hall doors swung open before them. There were only eight for the meal. The round table had been collapsed back into the memory store, and a plain Laothian dining mat spread in its place. Besides Tarli and Dom there were Joan, Keja, the Emperor, Sharli, Hrsh-Hgn and a small

216

dapper Laothian. The children's drosk servants stood behind them, and Isaac moved over to place himself behind Dom. He was holding Ig.

'Thanks,' said Dom, taking the creature. 'Where has he been? And how about you?'

'Just looking around the old place, boss. Ig's sort of the unofficial mascot of the bug-clearing crews – he can really root them out.'

Sharli looked up and blushed when Dom saw her.

The main course, kai shellfish, was eaten in silence, except for the efforts of a phnobic trio playing *chlong* at the other end of the hall.

A cool night breeze brought the tinkling of the leaves of the robot garden floating into the room.

The Emperor, with great ceremony, poured out a syrupy clear liquid that was deceptively light on the tongue and burned in the throat. The servants disappeared at a handclap. The trio hurried to the end of a phrase, unstrung their instruments and hurried away.

'Now,' said the Emperor. 'Let us talk.'

'Spies?' murmured Joan, into her glass. The Emperor raised his eyebrows.

'But of course, my dear,' he said. 'Over there the *inq*-player in the trio deposited an Ear before he left, my son's drosk servant reports regularly to their unpronounceable planet, and this room swarms with bugs and pinpoints. This very gentleman on my left' – the dapper man smiled – 'is an accomplished spy. His name is Magane.

One of his many jobs is to spy upon me. He reports to me regularly in case I act ill-advisedly. Where is Jokers World?' he ended abruptly.

Dom ran a finger round the edge of his glass.

'You have a mere seventy-two hours to discover it,' Ptarmigan prompted.

'That's unfair!' said Keja.

'He doesn't have to tell me.'

'I think I'm getting the idea,' said Dom mildly. 'I can feel the edges of a concept. The dark side of the sun . . . it's a bit non-committal, isn't it? Perhaps it refers to another set of dimensions?'

'You don't believe that,' said the Emperor. 'And neither do I. Jokers World is a singularity in this continuum. Probability suggests that this is the only universe in which they existed, although we can't locate them through math. My belief is that they were a billion-to-one chance that only cropped up in our particular space-time.'

'I think so too,' said Dom. 'There are only four to five examples of life apart from the races in the life-bubble, and they are big and – well, not life as we think of it. Like the Bank or Chatogaster. With them life is just another attribute, like mass or age. No, I think the Jokers were the first life-as-we-can-grasp-it in the galaxy, and I agree with the idea that they probably got our own shows on the road. I don't know why I agree. It just seems right.'

'I don't know about this idea,' said Keja. The Emperor smiled.

'You see, my dear, the universe has no time for life. By rights it shouldn't exist. We don't realize the odds.'

Dom nodded. 'We're so used to the idea of life as an essential part of the universe,' he said. 'Even in pre-Sadhim times we peopled other stars with imaginary beings and kidded ourselves that life off Earth was an odds-on chance. We didn't want to be alone.'

'Nor did the Jokersss,' said Hrsh-Hgn, leaning forward. 'So they altered chancess . . .'

'They peopled the stars too, only they must have been biological geniuses. They filled every ecological niche, too, from cool suns to frozen space . . .' Dom began. Then he stopped.

He knew about the Jokers. Other sentences thronged in his head, floated like icebergs in his mind. They had entered of their own accord – or had been put there.

He knew all about the Jokers. He *remembered* how they felt, surveying the empty planets, knowing the inbuilt block that every race ran up against eventually – the limitations of their evolutionary outlook . . .

He saw Jokers World, and sat stunned. The others carried on talking. The conversation coiled round him unheeded.

'The dark side of the sun sounds poetic,'

said Keja brightly. 'How about Screamer and Groaner?'

'The Internal Planettss of Protosstar Five?' said Hrsh-Hgn. 'Far too hot, and short-lived. They did not exist ten thousand yearss ago. So radio-active, too.'

'You're talking as if Jokers are human,' said Keja. 'It's never been proved. Couldn't they be silicoid? Look at the Creapii.'

'How about Rats?'

It was Tarli. He looked at their faces and shrugged.

'Well, we know what things are like on its planet. And the reversed-entropy situation might fit the Dark Side of the Sun saying.'

'The Creapii say any creatures on Tenalp can't possibly be intelligent,' said Ptarmigan sharply. 'And we'll have no more talk about that world in this place.'

'I think it's Earth,' said Joan firmly. The Emperor turned.

'That's a very homocentric statement. Can you justify it?'

She nodded. 'It's an old theory, after all. The Jokers were human, and I mean *human* human – sorry, Hrsh-Hgn, but you know what I mean – and they finally settled on Earth long before we were anything more than apes. They inter-bred with us eventually. Circumstantial evidence points to this. A lot of aliens consider the Jokers were human. Earth was the only planet apart from the Creapii homeworld to produce a race capable of reaching even its satellite . . . thirdly, Earthmen are the sort who would build something like the Chain Stars or the Centre of the Universe, just for the hell of it. Lastly, Earth is the home of the Joker Institute. It practically runs the planet. Half the directors of the Board of Earth are also in the Institute management committee. And the theory runs that the whole shooting match is run by a clique of pureblooded Jokers as a sly way of thwarting Joker studies. They have made attempts on Dom's life, for their ridiculous reasons. They don't want Jokers World found by anyone, but themselves.'

Hrsh-Hgn coughed. 'I sshould point out that ssimilar theoriess have been current with phnobes, drosks, Creapii, tarquins, sspoonerss and a sscore of otherss. Every race sseess itsself in the Jokerss. The Creapii ssay, who but Creapii could amasss the knowledge to capture the Centre of the Universse? The phnobess ssay, who but phnobes would have the insight into Totality to fasshion the Chain Sstars sso perfectly? The sspoonerss say, who but such ass we could have the *reimtole* into *gramepe* to sset the Maze? The tarquins broadcast, who but—'

'Point made,' said the Emperor.

'There is only one Sun in the universe,' said Dom.

They watched him struggle with his thoughts. 'It's simple,' he said, and looked perplexedly at

221

their expressions. 'There are plenty of stars, but the real Sun, the red bright thing is intelligent life.'

It was tantalizingly close. He saw through them and beyond the room, into the cosmopolitan world of the fifty-two known races, and inside that, snug as the yolk in the egg, the world of the Jokers on the dark side of the sun.

He wondered if the knowledge was being fed into his mind, and decided against it. He could provide too clear a chain of reasoning. All the loose ends tied up neatly, just like in a good probability math equation.

He had thought his father went knowingly to his death, as a good probability mathemagician should do. But his father had also been going to . . .

He heard a damp sizzle. Someone said: 'This really is too bad.' Someone was standing in the doorway.

Ways frowned into the muzzle of his molecule stripper and stepped further into the room.

'Good evening, Your Eminence, and assembled gentry. Now, at this point someone usually makes an impassioned call for the guard.'

The walls disappeared. Three guards fired at Ways simultaneously, and disappeared in clouds of light dust.

'The essence of the molecule stripper is the little matrix engine which can, in very rare circumstances, arc over and reverse the field,' said Ways. 'I believe that just happened.'

The Emperor recovered first. He poured out more wine, proffered the glass to Ways, and smiled thinly.

'Would you explain how you got in?' he said. 'I must review our alarm system.'

'Certainly. I brought my ship down on the terrace. I expect most of your alarms failed.'

'You are lucky,' said Ptarmigan mildly.

'I was built so. You made me, in fact.'

'Ah yes. Luck as an electronic faculty. I remember supervising the plans myself. What a pity we didn't think of incorporating some kind of switch.'

'It wouldn't have worked,' said Ways. 'But enough of this chitter-chatter. How can I kill Dom Sabalos, who is invulnerable? If I dropped a rock on his head Brownian motion would contrive to knock it off course.'

Sharli swung her *koto*. It flashed towards Ways' chest and collapsed like tinfoil. She stared at it in disbelief.

'Don't worry,' he said. 'A statistically possible chance can happen to anyone. Excuse me.' He drew a simple United Spies official-issue assassination gun and fired at Dom again.

The bullet stopped in mid-air and boiled.

A faint tremor ran round the universe.

'Molecular resistance,' said Ways. 'Damn.' He sat down on the mat and took up the glass of wine. He smiled at them, and gestured with the stripper.

'There must be a hundred more ships up there,' he said. 'Phnobic, drosk, Creap, Spooner, Pod. All watching this place and each other. How many planets in this system, Your Eminence?'

'Since the First Sirian Bank shot out of his orbit and into interspace, I expect there are now six,' said Ptarmigan.

'Correct. The Bank is now in orbit forty million miles out beyond – what's the name of your outermost world?'

'Far Out,' said Tarli.

'So you see, everyone feels a burning interest in Dom's moves during the next few days. Me too. The arrangements have been modified slightly. We are all going to Jokers World.'

He waved them into silence. 'Dom and I are lucky. He is protected – by the Jokers, it is believed – while my luck is genuine silicon-chip certain. However, I am afraid the rest of you aren't lucky. Do I make my point? The terms "hostage" and "kill" are unsavoury, and therefore I will not use them . . .'

A mechanical bat wheeled into the dusk as they trooped across the terrace. Ways' little ship was there. It was small, small enough to have its shape dictated by the single matrix engine it contained. A saddle for the pilot and a frame for the auxiliary equipment were wrapped over the front of the coil, and landing gear was simply welded onto the engine housing. It was a machine for getting from place to place with the minimum of comfort and the maximum of efficiency – and it was fast. It had no name.

Dom climbed into the saddle, closed the transparent housing and inspected the controls. Ways' voice with its final instructions was muffled by the plastic.

'Let us be quite clear. Should I lose contact with you, or should you make any improper move, I shall be forced to take steps. Wait for us in orbit.'

The ship lifted smoothly. Once out of atmosphere Dom could survey most of the Tau Ceti system on the tiny scanner screen. The ships showed up as blue pinpoints. A long way out was something else – the scanner kept flickering from red to blue as the Class Two brain built into it tried to decide whether it was a ship or a world. As Dom watched, the blip disappeared. The Bank had ducked into interspace. Dom remembered seeing the huge matrix engine in one of the caverns. It wouldn't take much to float a planet.

Ten minutes later the *Drunk With Infinity* was a bright star over Laoth's terminator. Ways had chosen a good ship. Dom set up the co-ordinates he had been given on the matrix computer and sighed.

The jump was short, lasting barely half an hour subjective time. It ended in the middle of a fleet.

Ways said: 'Open up the communicator circuits.'

He saw the main cabin of the *Drunk*, with the hostages standing mutely in the middle of the floor. Most were, at least. Joan I was being supported, and Isaac was sprawled on the floor.

Ways walked into the field of view. 'I've run into a little pocket of resistance,' he said. 'Don't let that worry you.'

'What's the fleet for?' said Dom.

'Company. Who knows if we may have to fight, survey, or merely land on a dead world?'

Dom laughed hysterically in the tiny cabin, and stopped only when he saw Ig cowering away on the control panel and gazing at him in wide-eyed terror.

'You're fools,' he told the communicator. 'You think I will lead you to a planet?'

The scene of the *Drunk* flickered out, and another face looked at him. It was thin, topped off by a mop of black hair, and had unmistakably been born on Earth.

'I am sorry about this,' it said. 'My name is Franz Asman, of the Joker Institute. This is our fleet. Ways is our tool.'

'Earthman, eh?' said Dom. 'That means you don't really think the threat of reprisals is enough to stop me running away. An Earthman would let his grandmother fry if he saw any personal profit in it.'

'Sadhim preserve us from interworld animosity,' said Asman wearily. 'As a matter of fact, you know, I've been studying you for some time. There's a staff of two hundred at the Institute who have been studying you for some time, too. We know exactly what you will do in any given situation, and in this one you won't run.'

'Studying me?' Behind Asman's head he could see vague figures, in front of a long panel covered with intricate patterns of coloured lines.

'This is our job. Do you know what an astrologer was?'

'Sure,' said Dom. 'I was born under O'Brien the Hunter.'

'We are the new astrologers. We evaluate—'

—by the mathemagic of probability, sifting through the population of the galaxy to find those whose probability profile matched the theoretical one for the discoverer of Jokers World. That particular profile had been in existence for some time. For no known reason questions relating to Jokers World usually became nonsense when rendered into p-math, but it was possible, just possible, to make up an equation from the outlines round the logical holes.

Then it meant sifting again. That had not been difficult. There were only three potential discoverers this year. One was a phnobic monk, the other a three-month-old girl on Third Eye. Both had been killed easily.

But Dom was a different matter. The Institute was at a loss to understand why. His father had also been a high-probability Discoverer, and there had been no difficulty there. Yet something prevented Dom from being conveniently removed. He was too lucky.

Something wanted him to discover Jokers World.

'Yes,' said Dom. 'It's the Jokers.'

'So we think,' said Asman. 'Do you know why we can't let you?'

'I think I can follow your reasoning,' said Dom. 'You fear the Jokers. That's because you don't know them. You think that contact with even the remnants of their culture will destroy us. I expect you have some idea that men are better off without gods.'

'You laugh at us. Oh, we can't deny that the Joker artefacts have done something to stimulate interracial co-operation.'

Dom heard himself shout: 'They caused it! The Creapii invented the matrix engine just so that they could find other lifeforms to help them answer the Joker riddles!'

'That is so. But Dom, listen. Before Sadhim, before star travel even, you know that most men believed in some kind of omnipresent god? Not the Sadhimist Small Gods, answerable to natural forces, but a real Director of the Universe? But if it had turned out that He really did exist chaos would have been let loose on the planet. He would have ceased to become a matter of comforting Belief but a matter of fact – you don't *believe* in the sun, either. And men would have perished of a cosmic inferiority complex. You can't live and *know* of such greatness.

'We need the idea of Jokers because they are a unifying force among the races, but we can't afford to find their world. Supposing it is dead – is that the end of even the greatest race? If they still live, will they enslave us or ignore us? Or worse, befriend us?

'We can only let you go now to the dark side of the sun. But you must understand that we can't let you return.'

'I know what the Jokers World is,' said Dom slowly. 'I've known for some time, I think, without realizing it. And I think I'm coming to realize where it is. There is only one Sun in the universe – our universe – and the Jokers gave it to us. Will you lock your fleet onto this ship?'

Asman nodded.

'Then follow me.'

Interspace glowed around him. Dom switched off the set and tried to ignore the orange-gold glow that filled the ship and in which it floated.

To no one he said: 'Why now? And why me?'

Ig shrugged, and turned his pointed, rat-like nose towards him. He spoke. The words arrived in Dom's head without the need for a cumbersome physical route.

'The trouble was that we never found a way to become empathic. Telepathy – that's merely a higher form of speech. But to know how another being, another creature feels – that is impossible.'

'You were lonely,' said Dom. 'All those empty years . . .'

'Isaac would say: close, but no cigar. We searched even the alternate universes, it is true, right along to the dark impossible ones that are the stuff of nightmares. There was life. The Bank and Chatogaster are small fry. In some universes the very suns live. There is a galaxy that sings. In one universe, over there' – a paw pointed and one claw disappeared momentarily into another continuum – 'there is nothing but thought, which pervades all. Not only thought, but understanding. But it is alien to us. How blithely you use the word alien: you have no idea how alien a thing may be.

'We discovered – as the Creapii are discovering – that the ultimate barrier is one's viewpoint. Dimly they realize that even their most objective statements about the universe cannot be freed from the Creapii taint because they ultimately derive from Creapii minds and emotions. That's why they are the great ambassadors of inter-racial harmony, and why they try so hard to be everything but Creapii.'

'So you invented us,' said Dom. 'At least that

theory is true? You wanted to get, uh, different points of view?'

'Close again. All we had to do was make it easier for intelligent life to evolve. That at least is not difficult; it's well within the range of your sciences. Though it was damn difficult to hit the right combination for cold-helium life. By the way, I have a small bomb surgically implanted in me. The Earthmen did it. Very subtle. I wouldn't worry; I have inactivated it.'

Ig paused and scratched an ear.

'We left artefacts to tantalize,' he said. 'I'm afraid we cheated. Be sure that before we left we were very thorough in cleaning up the galaxy. On some worlds we had to build an entirely new crust, down to the fossils. We had to replace metals in the grounds as ores, replenish oilfields, relay coal measures – we wanted to make sure you had a start in life. We gave you reconditioned worlds, but we left you the Towers and the Chain Stars and so on. All cultural fakes, I'm afraid. Made to awe rather than inform. But we had to leave the clue. That was artistically correct.'

'The dark side of the sun,' said Dom. 'It was two clues. If you hadn't wanted us to translate it, we never would have done. That was clue one. After all, we couldn't even have translated Phnobic without the phnobes there to help us out. And the sun – you turned your back on intelligence, and became dull-minded animals.'

'Please! Swamp igs are reasonably bright, considering their environment. We selected our new selves with care. Believe me, it is pleasant to have no enemies and to lie in the warm mud. We had to build in safeguards – a genetic twist to make us lucky animals, so that we were venerated rather than hunted. And an alarm, so that when the time came we would remember. These little bodies have made good hiding places.'

'I'll just ask again: why me?' said Dom.

'You live at the right time. You are naturally cosmospolitan. You come from Widdershins. That *was* our world, once. Long ago, of course. You are rich, there is a certain amount of glamour attached to your position. Let's say it was fate.'

He squinted through the canopy at the glowing, heatless fires of interspace.

'Excuse me,' said Dom. 'But you don't look like a super-race.'

Ig's paws were darting rapidly across the console of the matrix computer. He looked up and stared at Dom—

—Dom rubbed his eyes. 'I'm sorry,' he said. A few seconds later he tried to remember what he had seen during that moment of contact, but it had gone now, leaving only an impression of greatness and understanding.

'Thank you,' said Ig quietly. 'You see, people expect an advanced race to land in golden ships and say, "Throw away your weapons, cease fighting among yourselves, and join the great galactic brotherhood." It isn't like that. Young races do that.'

'What happens now?'

'Now?'

. . . we will meet you, came the thought. Together, perhaps, we will see the universe as it really is. And when we meet you, we will do so as equals. We are all mere subspecies of the one race of bright sun dwellers, after all. And the whole is infinitely greater than the sum of the parts. Now . . .

'Now,' said Ig, 'we will talk.'

The fleet hung against the shimmering bulk of Widdershins. Other ships were flashing into existence all through the system, as the followers homed in on the interspace shadow. The radio was a gabble of many tongues.

'They're going to fight it out!' moaned Joan. 'Oh my God, they're going to fight!'

The control deck of the Earth command ship was dominated by the big state-of-space circle-screen. They watched the incoming ships form a rough pattern. Their commanders had been doing some very rapid diplomacy.

Asman walked over from one of the control desks, shaking his head.

'I'm sorry,' he began. 'Widdershins, eh? Are you Widdershines Jokers, then? You were only a small colony to begin with, it's not inconceivable . . .'

The ship trembled. Something was rising out of interspace, a great bulk with a voice that boomed through the pick-up system.

'HO THERE! I WILL PROSECUTE ECONOMIC SANCTIONS AGAINST THE FIRST RACE TO MAKE AN AGGRESSIVE ACT!'

The Bank took up a watchful orbit closer in towards See-Why.

Dom slid back the hatch of the small ship and stepped out into space.

He walked carefully, unsure of his footing, and stopped a dozen metres from the ship. The faintest of shimmers hung around him. He was holding something in his outstretched hands.

Ig stood up on his ridiculous hind pair of legs and spoke.

In the command ships lights dimmed, circuitry blew out and the walls trembled to the roar of the sound.

There was a short pause. Then the little Joker lowered his voice. The message was clearer then, but almost as devastating. It was: *Land. We, the Jokers, the galaxy-striders, the star-shapers, ask it.*

You have a great deal to teach us.

*   *   *

After a struggle Dom pacified the wild windshell and coaxed it around towards the shore.

Five miles away, by the joke that was the Jokers Tower, more ships were landing. Quietly, trying to avoid catching each other's visual apparatus, the fifty-two races were making their way into the swamp.

Dom had left Ig seated in the mud, the focus of a wide and growing ring of listeners. And other Igs were dog-paddling along the water lanes. Something new was going to happen to the universe. It would involve all the races. They were, after all, only aspects of the one great race of thinking creatures – the dwellers on the bright side of the sun. It would take time, but one day something would come back out of interest to Widdershins, in the dank swamp, and say: it began here.

But just for once – for twice – Dom was playing truant. Though there was still one duty to perform. Balancing on the rocking shell he removed the stopper from the small bottle and tipped its contents into the sea. Then carefully, to avoid the shell's stings, he stuck his head into the water to hear, far off and faint, the words *Thank you* in sea-noise.

He looked back to the distant beach. A figure had wandered down to the surf line, wrapped in a golden glow. She was watching him thoughtfully.

Dom urged the shell through the breakers. Now, he thought, we will listen.

THE END

GOOD OMENS

by Terry Pratchett & Neil Gaiman

According to the Nice and Accurate Prophecies of Agnes Nutter – the world's only *totally reliable* guide to the future – the world will end on a Saturday. Next Saturday, in fact. Just after tea . . .

'A superbly funny book. Pratchett and Gaiman are the most hilariously sinister team since Jekyll and Hyde. If this is Armageddon, count me in'
James Herbert

'GOOD OMENS is frequently hilarious, littered with funny footnotes and eccentric characters. It's also humane, intelligent, suspenseful, and fully equipped with a chorus of "Tibetans, Aliens, Americans, Atlanteans and other rare and strange creatures of the Last Days." If the end is near, Pratchett and Gaiman will take us there in style'
Locus

'Wickedly funny'
Time Out

'Hilarious Pratchett magic tempered by Neil Gaiman's dark steely style; who could ask for a better combination?'
Fear

0 552 13703 0

THE DISCWORLD NOVELS OF TERRY PRATCHETT

THE FUNNIEST AND MOST UNORTHODOX FANTASIES IN THIS OR ANY OTHER GALAXY

THE COLOUR OF MAGIC

On a world supported on the back of a giant turtle (sex unknown), a gleeful, explosive, wickedly eccentric expedition sets out. There's an avaricious but inept wizard, a naïve tourist whose luggage moves on hundreds of dear little legs, dragons who only exist if you believe in them, and of course THE EDGE of the planet . . .

'One of the best, and one of the funniest English authors alive'
Independent

The Colour of Magic is the first novel in the now legendary *Discworld* series.

0 552 12475 3

TERRY PRATCHETT'S FAMOUS *DISCWORLD* SERIES NOW AVAILABLE ON TAPE!

Twenty-seven titles in the now legendary *Discworld* series are available in Corgi audio.

'Pure fantastic delight' *Time Out*

Each title comes abridged on two tapes lasting approximately three hours.

A LIST OF OTHER TERRY PRATCHETT TITLES AVAILABLE FROM CORGI BOOKS

THE PRICES SHOWN BELOW WERE CORRECT AT THE TIME OF GOING TO PRESS. HOWEVER TRANSWORLD PUBLISHERS RESERVE THE RIGHT TO SHOW NEW RETAIL PRICES ON COVERS WHICH MAY DIFFER FROM THOSE PREVIOUSLY ADVERTISED IN THE TEXT OR ELSEWHERE.

☐	12475 3	THE COLOUR OF MAGIC	£6.99
☐	12848 1	THE LIGHT FANTASTIC	£6.99
☐	13105 9	EQUAL RITES	£5.99
☐	13106 7	MORT	£6.99
☐	13107 5	SOURCERY	£5.99
☐	13460 0	WYRD SISTERS	£6.99
☐	13461 9	PYRAMIDS	£6.99
☐	13462 7	GUARDS! GUARDS!	£6.99
☐	13463 5	MOVING PICTURES	£6.99
☐	13464 3	REAPER MAN	£6.99
☐	13465 1	WITCHES ABROAD	£6.99
☐	13890 8	SMALL GODS	£6.99
☐	13891 6	LORDS AND LADIES	£6.99
☐	14028 7	MEN AT ARMS	£6.99
☐	14029 5	SOUL MUSIC	£6.99
☐	14235 2	INTERESTING TIMES	£6.99
☐	14236 0	MASKERADE	£6.99
☐	14237 9	FEET OF CLAY	£6.99
☐	14542 4	HOGFATHER	£6.99
☐	14598 X	JINGO	£6.99
☐	14614 5	THE LAST CONTINENT	£6.99
☐	14615 3	CARPE JUGULUM	£6.99
☐	14616 1	THE FIFTH ELEPHANT	£6.99
☐	14768 0	THE TRUTH	£5.99
☐	14840 7	THIEF OF TIME	£6.99
☐	14161 5	THE STREETS OF ANKH-MORPORK (with Stephen Briggs)	£8.99
☐	14324 3	THE DISCWORLD MAPP (with Stephen Briggs)	£8.99
☐	14608 0	A TOURIST GUIDE TO LANCRE (with Stephen Briggs and Paul Kidby)	£6.99
☐	14672 2	DEATH'S DOMAIN (with Paul Kidby)	£8.99
☐	14673 0	NANNY OGG'S COOKBOOK (with Stephen Briggs, Tina Hannan and Paul Kidby)	£8.99
☐	14429 0	MORT – THE PLAY (adapted by Stephen Briggs)	£4.99
☐	14430 4	WYRD SISTERS – THE PLAY (adapted by Stephen Briggs)	£4.99
☐	14431 2	GUARDS! GUARDS! – THE PLAY (adapted by Stephen Briggs)	£6.99
☐	14432 0	MEN AT ARMS – THE PLAY (adapted by Stephen Briggs)	£6.99
☐	14159 3	THE LIGHT FANTASTIC – GRAPHIC NOVEL	£9.99
☐	14556 4	SOUL MUSIC: THE ILLUSTRATED SCREENPLAY	£9.99
☐	14575 0	WYRD SISTERS: THE ILLUSTRATED SCREENPLAY	£9.99
☐	13325 6	STRATA	£6.99
☐	13703 0	GOOD OMENS (with Neil Gaiman)	£6.99
☐	52595 2	TRUCKERS	£4.99
☐	52586 3	DIGGERS	£4.99
☐	52649 5	WINGS	£4.99
☐	52752 1	THE CARPET PEOPLE	£4.99
☐	13926 2	ONLY YOU CAN SAVE MANKIND	£4.99
☐	52740 8	JOHNNY AND THE DEAD	£4.99
☐	52968 0	JOHNNY AND THE BOMB	£4.99
☐	54693 3	THE AMAZING MAURICE AND HIS EDUCATED RODENTS	£5.99

All Transworld titles are available by post from:

Bookpost, PO Box 29, Douglas, Isle of Man IM99 1BQ

Credit cards accepted. Please telephone 01624 836000, fax 01624 837033, Internet http://www.bookpost.co.uk or e-mail: bookshop@enterprise.net for details.

Free postage and packing in the UK. Overseas customers allow £1 per book (paperbacks) and £3 per book (hardbacks).